UNHARMONIOUS

To Andrea,

Read this book first!

Thanks for your support.

Liane Bayh

November 2015

Ballad Publishing
Lincoln, Nebraska

UNHARMONIOUS

LAINE BOYD

Ballad
Publishing

Book design copyright 2014 by Ballad Publishing. All rights reserved.
Cover design and interior design by Ballad Publishing
Cover illustration by Theresa Ann
Romance Fatal Serif font by Juan Casco

Published by Ballad Publishing Company
PO Box 6193
Lincoln, NE 68506, USA

Ballad Publishing Company and the "MANDOLIN" logo are trademarks of
Ballad Publishing Company or an affiliated company

Library of Congress Control Number: 2014947950

Published in the United States of America
ISBN-13: 978-0-9899689-2-8
ISBN-10: 0989968928
1. Fiction/Suspense/Thriller/Music/Symphony
2. Fiction/Mystery/Suspense/Music

Coming soon from Laine Boyd

Dinner and a Murder

To my husband, Bryan, the love of my life, for his faithful, loving support and cheerful encouragement.

ACKNOWLEDGEMENTS

I am deeply grateful to the following people, whose specialized knowledge and insight provided invaluable help: Lynn Hague, violist, St. Louis Symphony Orchestra; Officer Steven Devore, Jefferson County Police; Sandi Hafner, Registered Nurse; and Attorney Gary H. Lange. Their expertise in their respective fields and willingness to take the time to answer a myriad of questions lends not only credibility to the story, but provided an educational experience for me as well. I hope that I have done justice to the information my sources provided to me. If I have not been as accurate as I should have been, or taken too much liberty with certain scenes in this story, the fault lies with me and not with those who were so generous with their time and willingness to help me.

Gloria Harrison, Kris Hillen, Sandi Hafner, Kim Reno, Christy Reno and Bryan Boyd provided support as test readers. Their excitement was contagious and encouraging.

Reverend John Hancock and his wife, Margaret, who from my youth modeled Christian compassion, hospitality, with faith and love, provided inspiration for several of the characters in the book. In addition to raising their own children, they opened their home and their hearts to the poor and needy, taking in several Vietnamese boat people, including an entire family of four, and established lifelong friendships. Their example of sacrificial love made an indelible impression on me and countless others for whom their door was always open.

1

Rehearsal was finally, *finally* over. Julie Davenport packed her cello carefully and quickly made her exit, hurrying to her car.

"Julie! Oh, Julie! Oh, my dear, it's so nice to have you back with us. How are you, dear? You've been through such a terrible ordeal! So sad. We've been very worried about you, haven't we, Stanley?"

Julie Davenport smiled wanly at Stanley and Sheila Goldman, sighing to herself. She had hoped to leave rehearsal unnoticed for a hasty retreat home. But it was Stanley and Sheila, so she forced herself to be sociable. "It's good to be back. It's been a struggle, but I've got to join the land of the living sometime." She opened the back door of her white, late-model Maxima, carefully laid her cello on the back seat and strapped it in securely.

She didn't feel like talking to anyone, but found it impossible to be rude to Stanley and Sheila. He was elderly, possibly the oldest member of the symphony, and played the violin. When Julie first started at the SLSO, Stanley and his wife, Sheila, a violist, took Julie under their wing. They had always been kind and supportive of her and she was closer to them than anyone else in the symphony. Sheila did most of the talking and Stanley did most of the agreeing. Julie found them a comical, but loving pair, however, this was her first day back, and she wasn't in the mood for socializing.

"I need to get going. It's a long drive and I'm tired after being away from it all so long. Why don't we plan on lunch sometime after rehearsal?"

"Oh dear, that would be lovely. Wouldn't that be lovely, Stanley? Having lunch with Julie?"

"Yeah, Sheila, I heard you. Julie, doll, it's good to see you. We know you may need a little time, but we're here for you."

"Thanks." Julie gave them both a brief hug before getting into her car. She sighed heavily, waved to the Goldmans and pulled out of the parking lot.

She drove westbound on I-44 at a tame 55 miles per hour. Traffic at this time of day was light and there was no particular need to hurry; rush hour would not begin for another hour or more. Until then, the highway was relatively deserted, even in the city, but her commute began at Grand Avenue, still a little way from downtown St. Louis.

To her left and right, facing the highway were single-family homes, duplexes, and apartments in various stages, including none, of rehabilitation. These old neighborhoods still retained much of their character and the war on drugs had not yet been completely lost. St. Louis was a city brimming with charm and culture, where many families chose to either remain or put down new roots within its borders. Nevertheless, its problems were many and there was a continuing trend to move further west with hopes that the suburbs and beyond might provide fewer challenges.

She continued, passing through Webster Groves, Crestwood, Kirkwood and past I-270, leaving the city and its struggles behind, driving past the more affluent suburbs, still traveling westbound. The sweet strains of Mozart wafted through the car creating an atmosphere which lulled her into a not unpleasant frame of mind. The drive from the city to home seemed much shorter and far more enjoyable listening to the seemingly endless repertoire which Mozart left for future generations to relish.

As the car approached the 141-Fenton-Valley Park exit, which most St. Louisans considered the last bastion of civilization, the Maxima's speed steadily increased to 65, and car and driver headed still further west on I-44 into the densely tree covered hills announcing home.

Julie relaxed. It would not be long before she arrived at the exit which led into the woods in these foothills of the Ozark Mountains. Home.

St. Louis at this time of year was fragrant and green. This particular June had been unseasonably cool and surprisingly, not as humid as usual. The trees were bursting with the fullness of their rich and varied green colors as their majestic arms reached toward heaven to glorify their Creator. Julie smiled as they greeted her. She felt inspired, blessed by the beauty that summer was pouring down, and basked in its wonder. These trees; on the left, Forest 44 and the right, Lone Elk Park, were home to hawks, owls, whippoorwills, cardinals, bluebirds and a myriad of other feathered creatures. Chipmunks and squirrels took up residence in them and deer, fox and even an occasional bear found shelter beneath their protective limbs. This serene stretch of I-44 was peaceful and Julie enjoyed entertaining the idea that this part of Missouri remained virtually untouched since the dawn of creation.

Of course, it hadn't, but many St. Louisans referred to it as The Land That Time Forgot and in some ways, that description was correct. In spite of the rabid development that raped the scenic landscape throughout much of the St. Louis area, this rough and rocky expanse was still sparsely populated. It was this natural beauty, raw and undisturbed that kept Julie from living closer to work, friends, and other activities. The long drive home seemed a small sacrifice to pay for the pleasure she derived from living in a semi-wilderness that was at least relatively close to the city.

At last, the Maxima approached the exit which would eventually wind through even more densely wooded, twisting roads. Roads that wound in every conceivable direction; up, down, and around and around, until even an experienced navigator could not keep track of which direction he might be headed without a compass. As the car pulled off the highway, Julie slowed in anticipation of the treacherous course which lay ahead. It was utter foolishness to drive these narrow byways at an unsafe speed. Many a driver had been hurled into eternity after missing a curve and careening off the side of a mountain or smashing headlong into a stately, centuries-old tree. But for the unhurried driver, the danger was mitigated by the sheer beauty of nature that lined every twist and turn. From spring through the middle of autumn, the trees arched over the road, their foliage so thick the sun was blocked out, rendering the paths noticeably cooler in temperature.

Julie continued. So did Mozart.

Suddenly, a strange car appeared, seemingly from nowhere, looming in the rearview mirror. It had not been on the highway behind her. Julie was sure of that. For that matter, there had been no other cars on the highway once she passed the 141 exit. She also knew there were no other exits onto this little traveled back road. Julie considered herself familiar with the cars that traveled on her isolated route and she was certain this was not one of them. There were few neighbors out here, and this car, an older, green Buick, did not belong to any of them.

She slowed and pulled far to the right for the Buick to pass, but it hung back. Julie increased her speed. Even though she knew these paths by heart, she had no desire to drive over the speed limit. The green Buick increased its speed to match that of the Maxima's. Past each turnoff, up hills and down, around every curve, the Maxima could not lose the Buick. Its driver was relentless in his pursuit of the small white car. Beads of sweat dampened Julie's forehead when the realization set in that this unknown car was indeed in pursuit. *Who on earth is following me and why?* She began to feel dizzy and tried not to panic.

The closer she got to home, the more desperate she became to lose her stalker. She certainly did not want to lead him to her house. With a sudden burst of speed and the turn-off to home coming up, the Maxima took off, flying over bumps and potholes, momentarily leaving the Buick behind. Coming up was the widest turn in the road, followed by a series of small hills. This was the only chance for Julie to get far enough ahead of the

Buick so its driver could not see which way she would go. She accelerated more, silently praying she would not lose control of her car. The driver of the Buick, too unfamiliar with the lay of the land, was unable to keep up. At speeds the Maxima had never attained on these roads, it reached the little worn, well-disguised, grass and dirt covered turnoff that would take her to the safety of home. Screeching and feeling she was surely on two wheels, Julie, fearful of overturning, turned the car off the main thoroughfare and raced up the side of the mountain into a copse of trees where the road below could be watched without danger of the observer being seen.

Well hidden, the Maxima stopped. Julie stepped out, breathing hard, her heart racing, to watch for the Buick, her electric blue eyes earnestly searching the road below, her long, dark red curls blowing back from her pale face. She saw it drive past her turnoff and disappear over the hills, only to return a few minutes later. For the next several minutes, it drove back and forth on the road below, and then angrily sped off back toward the highway.

She stood by her car a few more moments, perplexed, and finally breathed a deep sigh of relief as her heart rate returned to normal. She could not believe someone would have followed her and then continued the search after being outrun. She could not imagine why anyone would come after her, but at any rate, she had escaped. In grand style. *I should have been a stunt car driver.*

She tried to calm herself. She pressed her fingers into her eyebrows, closed her eyes and continued her monologue in an attempt to regain her composure. *Calm, calm, calm. It's all right to talk to yourself, as long as you don't answer yourself.*

Returning to the present, she carefully checked her precious cargo safely strapped in the back seat. Her cello, nestled snugly within its hard case, had not moved through the drive home. Her instrument, which was priceless to her, suffered no apparent damage, but she would check it thoroughly when she got home. After remaining a few more minutes to be certain her pursuer was not returning, she climbed back into the driver's seat, still shaken, and carefully completed the remaining trek to her driveway. She pushed the button opening the garage door and pulled her Maxima in beside Jack's dark green Jaguar.

Coming home was now a tangle of mixed emotions. This beautiful home, which she loved, had been Jack's wedding gift to her; custom built to the last minute detail, he had surprised and thrilled her when he first brought her here.

They were driving in the Jaguar, its hunter green color gleaming in the sun, the tan leather interior luxurious and comfortable. Julie felt as if they had been driving forever.

"Where are we going sweetheart?" she had purred softly to him.

Jack only smiled. "You'll see."

The trunk was full of their honeymoon luggage and enough souvenirs to stock a Wal-Mart. Julie was happier and more content than she could ever remember being. She leaned back into the seat and sighed lazily, looking forward to more of the same marital bliss that had been theirs for two weeks.

Eventually, Jack turned off the road onto what looked to Julie like no path at all, only woods and headed up a mountain pass to an enormous home, a modern day castle of cedar, stone, and glass. A horseshoe driveway wound between huge, stone pillars connected to the entryway by a domed canopy, and wound in the other direction toward the five-car garage at the back of the house.

Jack pulled up to the front and parked under the cedar canopy. The views were spectacular from everywhere on this mountain top property and Julie was wide-eyed and lightheaded as she took it all in.

"Where are we, Jack? What is this place?"

"We're home, darling. Do you like it?"

"*Here?*" she stuttered. "I…I thought we were going to stay in my condo in the Central West End. That's what we talked about, you know, until we found a house to buy…Oh, Jack, this is just beautiful. I…I don't know what to say. This is so far out of St. Louis, oh, but it's gorgeous, I love it, I really do. I just don't know what to say. Oh, I already said that, didn't I, but I don't! This wasn't what we planned, you know, the condo…I just…I just…" She was stammering, talking a mile a minute and not making any sense at all. She felt stupid and inadequate. Jack had built her a magnificent dream home, completely taking her by surprise and her response was incoherent as she mumbled about her condo in the city's stylish Central West End. Embarrassed, she finally shut up.

She looked up at Jack, tall, lean and handsome, afraid she had offended him on their first day back from their fairytale, romantic honeymoon, but he was smiling at her, his deep blue eyes sparkling in amusement.

"Well, darling," he sighed, "we could tear it down and start all over again if it doesn't suit Your Highness perfectly, even though you haven't even seen the inside yet. Or, we can always go back to your cozy, little condo and hit the want ads in *The Post*. Maybe find a little something in a subdivision with as many as three or four different floor plans to choose from where the houses fit six to an acre. Unless, sweet love of my life, you have a better idea. Do tell, darling, I'm all ears. Where does my princess desire to make her abode?" He enjoyed teasing her and she could feel the color rising in her cheeks.

"Stop it, or I'll see to it that you live in a tent from now on." She hugged him tightly and reached up for the kiss she knew was waiting for her. "It's perfectly wonderful and you know it, Jack Davenport. I love this house and I love you. But why didn't you tell me about this? How could you keep such a big secret from me? Some love of your life I am!"

"This is your wedding gift. I wanted to give you something unforgettable."

"You've already given me plenty," Julie muttered, barely audible, their honeymoon still fresh in her memory. "And besides, I gave you diamond cuff links and studs. They rather pale in comparison, I think."

"They were exquisite, darling. Not quite as exquisite as you, of course, but exquisite, nonetheless." His faintly British accent could still make Julie giddy. She loved listening to her husband's voice, smooth and soothing. Everything he did was smooth. Jack seemed so perfect. And he loved her.

"Well. Let's see the inside. Maybe it won't be as horrid as the outside," she teased. "So, Mr. Smarty Pants, if you did anything right, then maybe I won't insist that you tear the whole thing down after all." She started for the front door.

"Hold on, Your Majesty," he said, pulling her back. "If this house was back East…"

"Oh, like Mr. Europe knows all about back East!"

He put his hand over Julie's mouth, the best way to ever silence her, and continued. "Like I was saying before I was so *rudely* interrupted, if this house was back East, we would have to name it. I intend to be fully American here, therefore, I want us to choose a name before we go inside. Come on, let's walk around the property before we go in and properly christen all the rooms, which, by the way, are numerous." A sly smile formed on his face and Julie blushed. "How about Eagle's Nest or Whispering Pines? There are hundreds of pine trees about, did you notice? What about Tall Oaks, or Del Vista? Davenport Manor, maybe?"

They were circling the mansion, all the while Julie wrinkling up her nose and making gagging noises at each of his suggestions, accusing him of watching too many soap operas.

"All right, princess, do share some of *your* bright ideas."

"I only have one, but since it is so bright, I only need one."

"Oh, drum roll, please…"

"I hereby christen this house…The Monstrosity."

"What! Juliette Davenport, for your information, the finest architects and construction crews in Europe and the States worked 'round the clock, seven days a week using the very highest quality materials with plenty of extra pay, I might add, so that your wedding present…"

"That's right," Julie interrupted. "*My* wedding present. *My* house. *My* choice of names. You can always take the tent, you know."

And so it was The Monstrosity. The intrepid Julie Davenport had spoken.

As Julie removed her cello from the back seat and started toward the door to the mud room, she gingerly stroked the fender of the Jaguar. Never again would she snuggle down into its plush leather seat while Jack confidently and expertly drove, one hand on the steering wheel, the other tenderly stroking her hair. Never again would she experience the tingling sensation that overcame her when he would pull off into a grove of trees and they would climb into the back seat like a couple of teenagers in the throes of a hormonal attack. Never again would her love find the expression it sought with the only man she had ever been with.

Jack was dead.

2

Captain Carlton Drake cornered Joe Spence behind a row of gunmetal gray file cabinets in the large office space filled with shelves, storage units, and cubicles. He did not waste time calling a formal meeting in his office. His tone was serious and his voice low.

"Joe, I want you to pick your team and get set up in Pineview. We have a rental not far from the center of town. It's a makeshift office, smaller than you're used to, but it will suffice. The sooner we close this case, the sooner you can return to St. Louis. Don't worry about the budget. You have the all clear to get whatever you need. This case is our number one priority." Captain Drake continued. "Introduce yourself to the local boys, but keep everything low-key. Be sure they know to keep our presence in Pineview under wraps. We don't want anyone to get suspicious of anything."

"What if some of the locals are involved?" Joe's knee-jerk reaction that nobody could be trusted reflected his careful, thorough approach to each assignment, and he knew the critical nature of this matter would push even his limit.

"I've run all the checks on the Pineview Police Department, if you can even call it that, and no red flags. Nobody looks suspicious. Pineview is a sleepy town and most of the folks have pretty much lived there for generations. You can take your pick of agents to go with you. I would suggest one other seasoned agent and one of the newbies, so you have somebody to take care of the grunt work while gaining valuable experience. If you need anyone else, let me know. When you think you're ready to close it up, call here for standby back-up ahead of time and we will be less than two minutes from you. Think about who you want, and choose carefully. Gather your team in the conference room in two hours for briefing."

"Yes, sir. Don't worry. We'll get it done."

Joe Spence didn't need two hours to choose his seasoned agent. Sam Hernandez was the best agent he knew and they had worked well together on several other cases in the past. He had complete confidence in Sam's intelligence, dedication, and professional demeanor. Sam had the best interrogation technique of anyone Joe had worked with in his twenty-plus years. Deciding on a probationary agent, however, was another matter. He looked over the list of the newbies, and decided immediately to go with one of the females. Their little office should have someone who could give the appearance of a secretary, and he felt a woman would be much more believable if anyone got nosy.

Keisha Livingston approached Joe and surprised him by bringing him a cup of coffee.

"Sir," she began. "I'm Keisha Livingston and I want the assignment."

Joe maintained his poker face. "What assignment is that, Ms. Livingston?" He was not aware his conversation with Captain Drake was within earshot of anyone.

"I know who you are going after and I want to be on your team. It's a big case, and I can work hard for you. I'm hungry to work on something important. I'd appreciate being given the chance. If I don't work out, send me back."

"Are you aware of exactly how dangerous this situation is? We are not going to work an eight hour day, go home, pop a beer, and watch television. We'll take enough time to sleep, and that's about it. This will be all we do until the job is done. It will not be easy. It is a difficult assignment. You won't be seeing your family, your boyfriend, your best friend, nobody."

"My family lives in Baltimore, I have no boyfriend, I'm not afraid of hard work, and I finished first in sharp shooting. I am a third degree black belt in six different schools of martial arts. I can type more than 75 words a minute, listen to hours of tape searching for a single clue, and decode, if necessary. I am willing to do whatever the job requires, whether it's something big or something seemingly insignificant. I will not complain about any work you give me. It's all important, and I want to be part of your team."

Joe kept his face still, showing no emotion, while he studied Keisha. He liked her persistence. She had moxie, but she also had manners. She exuded a quiet confidence without cockiness. Young and well groomed, she could easily look the part of a secretary. And she had everything he would have wanted, except experience. He thought she would work well with him and Sam. She was eager to please and Joe found her work ethic refreshing.

"Conference room, eleven o'clock sharp. Captain Drake will brief us."

Keisha Livingston smiled broadly, her teeth white as pearls against her dark, smooth skin. "Thank you, sir. You won't be sorry."

"Keisha. It's Joe. You will be working with me and Sam Hernandez, so we will call you Keisha and you will call us Sam and Joe. Got it?"

"Yes, sir, Joe."

Special Agent Samuel Hernandez was briefed by Joe Spence, and introduced himself to Keisha before the formal briefing. Teamwork was crucial for a successful outcome and he told Joe he was confident that Keisha was a good choice. The three of them entered the conference room together.

Captain Drake stood before the large, white drawing board looking at the two best agents in his department and the probie with the most promise. Joe could not have chosen better, and Captain Drake hoped all three would return safely when this was over. He took it very hard if he lost an agent, but it would be a blow to the bureau as well if his three best went down.

3

It had been over five months since Julie answered the door to two uniformed police officers. Before they had spoken a word, Julie knew her world was shattered.

Jack's Lear jet had experienced engine failure over the Rockies while he was en route on a business trip to California, crashed into a mountain and burned shortly after impact. Although local authorities in Colorado conducted the mandatory search for survivors, there was never any real hope of finding any. The fireball that resulted when the jet plummeted into the mountainside was too extensive; the fuselage, twisted and melted, became an instant grave for Jack Davenport, who always piloted alone. His body, what little of it was recovered, was burned beyond recognition, but DNA was run on a small scrap of clothing that had escaped the fire, and from that, Jack was identified.

The next few weeks were a blur. With Julie near the point of collapse, nameless, faceless friends whom she could not now remember, arranged Jack's memorial service and tried to comfort Julie, but her grief was beyond reach. She was numb with shock; nothing was real.

Everyone was wrong. Life didn't go on, couldn't go on without Jack. He was coming back, she told herself. He wasn't really dead. This was a mistake and everybody was wrong. He would never leave her. He would call her soon and apologize for this horrible mix-up. He would be able to explain everything, just like he always did. Nothing was going to change. He was going to walk through the door with flowers and comfort her, tell her how silly she was for believing all of these people who were wrong, *wrong*, *WRONG!*

But nothing of the sort happened, and slowly, the shock and disbelief lessened. Jack didn't call, didn't come home and his plane had, of course, been positively identified prior to Julie being notified.

Once Julie finally accepted that her beloved husband was indeed dead, but at least had not suffered, she could grieve. Her heart ached more than she knew was possible. She felt she could never recover, nor did she wish to. She stopped eating, and eventually stopped crying; she was simply out of tears. Her bones and muscles ached from agony. She slept for hours at a time at different times of the day, accepted no phone calls and wished her friends would all just go away. She didn't want their advice, detested their pity, and could not accept their comfort. Jack was gone forever. She would mourn his loss forever.

Her best friend from childhood, Su Li Tuan, put her arms around Julie and hugged her. She wanted to help her friend, but felt helpless. Julie was beyond consolation.

"Julie, do you want to talk to somebody? A counselor, maybe?"

"Why? Will a counselor bring him back? Make me feel better? No."

Su Li withdrew, looking downcast. Her shoulders slumped as she studied the floor.

"Oh, Su Li, I'm sorry. I know you are trying to help. I love you for the effort, but this black hole I'm in will not go away."

Su Li was quiet for a moment. Then her eyes became bright as she neared her friend again and took her hand. "Julie, I was thinking. Jack was a kind and generous man. He had many beautiful items of clothing. Do you think maybe Jack would want you to give his clothes to others who were less fortunate?"

Julie looked thoughtfully at her friend. The idea of giving Jack's things away was at first repugnant to her. She did not feel she could possibly part with anything that belonged to her beloved, but she realized Su Li's suggestion resonated with Jack's philanthropic heart.

"You know, you are right. Jack would want exactly that. It would be a good way to honor his memory. He would be proud of me. Su Li, you knew him well. That's a great idea. Jack always gave generously to charity. This is what he would want. Will you help me go through his things?"

"Of course. Keep a few special items for yourself. Pineview Community Church has an outreach ministry to those who are struggling. I am sure they would appreciate your donations and see that they reach those who need them most."

"That's a good idea, Su Li. Jack would be happy that I used his things to help others."

Julie and Su Li spent several days going through Jack's things until everything was boxed and ready to go.

"Jack sure didn't keep much in his pockets. I only found a few items. What should I do with them?"

"I'll put them away. Right now, I can't bear to part with anything, except that I know the clothes are going to a good cause."

"I'll run these up to the church for you, Julie," Su Li offered. She attended regularly and had often invited Julie to join her, an invitation Julie always politely declined.

"No. I think I will go. Maybe I can find some answers."

Julie left with the boxes piled in her back seat and trunk. There were a few cars in the church's parking lot so she assumed the building was open. She stepped inside and looked around the vestibule. On a bulletin board she saw pamphlets covering a wide array of topics, notices of youth events, concerts, etc. She began to thumb through a pamphlet on grieving, when a voice from behind startled her.

"Good morning. May I help you?"

Julie turned to see a tall, slender man in his fifties, graying at the temples, dressed in khakis and a t-shirt that said, "Christians aren't perfect, just forgiven," smiling at her. He glanced at the pamphlet in her hand.

"Oh. Um, hi." She spoke slowly, unsure of herself. "My name is Julie Davenport and I was wondering if your church might want some donations of men's clothing. They're out in the car."

"Julie Davenport," the man said thoughtfully, his brows furrowed, pursing his lips. He raised his eyebrows and opened his eyes wide. "Oh, my. Was your husband the man who was killed in the plane crash?"

Her eyes filled with tears as she nodded.

"Come in and sit down. I'm Judson Grady. I'm the pastor here." He led her to a comfortable chair in his office lined with books, plaques, photos, and memorabilia from numerous mission trips. He had a wall full of diplomas. Julie lost count of how many degrees the man had and wondered what he was doing in a little burg like Pineview. "I am terribly sorry for your loss. Can our church be of service to you in any way?"

"I just wanted to drop some things off," she answered. Then, no longer able to control her pain and anger, she lashed out, "How could a God of love take my husband like that?" She half expected Judson Grady to say one of the many stupid things she had heard since Jack's death. If God closes a window, He opens a door? Heaven needed one more angel, maybe? It was meant to be? She had heard every platitude and pat answer imaginable, so she braced herself for more.

Julie thought her abrupt manner may have offended Pastor Grady, and halfway didn't care, but she found him kind, genuine, and sympathetic.

"May I call you Julie?" She nodded and he continued, "Julie, we don't always know why God allows bad things to happen. The broad answer is because there is sin in the world, everyone suffers, and our suffering should bring us closer to God, but sometimes bad things happen to good people. It can be hard to understand, and for that matter, we may never understand.

If we were able to understand everything about God, then He wouldn't really be God, after all. He lets us see enough of who He is to get us through life, but we only get a very small glimpse of a very big God. We wouldn't be able to handle any more than that. Sometimes, you just have to hang on to what you do know, and let go of what you don't know."

"So, what do we know?"

"We know that God is good and He is good all the time. We know He is always wise and just. We know He does not make mistakes. We know He loves us beyond measure, and even though we may go through terrible trials and suffer loss, we are never alone, because He is always with us. The Lord never promised to keep us free from trouble or pain. But He did promise He would always be with us when we go through trouble and He shares in our pain."

"I feel very alone. I don't know how I can live without Jack."

"Julie, you are still grieving. Losing someone you deeply love is never something you get over. If anyone tells you that you will get over it, they are wrong. But you do get through it. There's a difference. God created us to feel, to relate to others and to Him. Give yourself some time, because quite simply, it takes time to work through grief. That's normal. But you are not alone, regardless of how you feel. You are never alone. God is right there beside you and you can trust that He has a plan for your life, even if you cannot see what that plan is right now. There is a difference between what we feel, as opposed to reality. The reality is that you can trust Him. In every circumstance."

"I have so many questions. I need answers."

"Julie, I don't mean to sound harsh, so I hope you don't take this the wrong way. But God does not owe us an explanation. He is perfect. We are not. I can tell you that there *are* answers to your questions, but I may not have them. And you may never find them. God may answer your questions in time, or, on the other hand, He may just tell you that you have to take a step of faith and trust that He knows what is best for you. I can't tell you that because I don't know God's will for your life. That's between you and Him."

Julie appreciated Pastor Grady's honesty. He had not been condescending toward her, or tried to soothe her with empty, flowery phrases. "Thanks for talking to me. I appreciate you taking the time. Can you help me unload the boxes?"

"Of course. We always appreciate donations and they will be put to good use, I can promise you that. Julie, the church is open every day and of course, we have services on Sunday. Please feel welcome to stop by any time."

She led him to the car and he seemed pleasantly surprised at the number of boxes to unload. It took them several trips. He thanked her again, gave her his card and reminded her that the door was always open. She drove away feeling a small measure of comfort mixed with uncertainty. Pastor Grady had given her much to think about and she pondered his words as she drove home.

When she arrived home, she sent a check to the church, certain it, too, would be put to good use. Maybe she would visit some time. Maybe Pastor Grady was right. She needed more time.

"Pretty girl, Judson. Who was she?" Kendra Grady slipped her arms around her husband and hugged him. Like him, she was gray at the temples, and had a kind manner. She could tell instantly when something was bothering her husband.

"Troubled girl, Kendra. She's lost her way, but we will bring her to the Lord in prayer and by His grace, He will be with her in her deepest need."

Julie withdrew into her work, her music. Music had insulated her once before from heartache and sorrow, when tragedy struck her family the first time, interrupting and permanently altering her childhood, and once again, music was the balm that slowly and methodically worked its healing touch, reaching to the depths of her grief-stricken soul.

For weeks she could practice nothing but scales. Her music, whether she was playing piano or cello, evoked too many emotions that she wanted and needed to keep buried deep within her. Scales elicited no particular feelings in Julie, and she mechanically went through them, octave after octave, safe within their sterility, until she achieved exhaustion.

After weeks of nothing but scales, Su Li entered the sanctuary of Julie's hallowed music room. "Julie, play your music. I realize scales are important, but I miss your music."

"I don't think I can play."

"Julie, you have a gift and you are robbing the world of it. You are robbing yourself. It's time."

Julie was silent. She did not want to admit Su Li was right, but Su Li tended to be right about a lot of things.

"Okay. Just because you are my best friend in the world."

She ventured to her music cabinet and pulled out some of her best loved pieces by Grieg, Debussy, Wagner, and her favorite composer for piano, Chopin. Although not aware of it at the time, it was the soothing Chopin *Prelude, Opus 28, Number 6*, in B minor that began to soften and heal Julie's pain. She played it slowly, as Chopin intended, only with repeat after repeat, expressing her sorrow, fingers to keys. After that, she played Beethoven's *Moonlight Sonata*, and began to work out her frustration on Grieg's *Piano Concerto in A Minor*. Back and forth, between cello and piano she played until her anguish reached a slow decrescendo, and Julie Davenport began to join the living, not quite whole, but at least no longer hollow inside. Once again, her music worked its magic. Her heart was healing and she was finally able to feel something other than pain.

It was June, five months after Jack's memorial service, when Julie returned to work, her dedication feverish and her mind singular in purpose.

The St. Louis Symphony Orchestra had been the center of her life before she met Jack. As a sophomore at Horton Watkins High School in Ladue, a wealthy suburb of St. Louis, Julie auditioned for and made the St. Louis Youth Symphony as a promising young cellist. Music was her life, her entire world, until Jack, and music was the only home to which she could return.

Born Juliette Glynne Creighton, the gifted first child of Dr. John Gregory Creighton, a prominent, successful surgeon and Anne Lowell Creighton, a concert pianist who tailored her career to piano teaching once she started her family, Julie was an only child for the first three years and eight months of her life. By the time her younger brother Philip was born, Julie was already in her second piano book. Her mother, recognizing Julie's ability to sing in tune at an unusually early age and pick out melodies on the piano, carefully nurtured her interest in music.

Julie was a quiet, thoughtful child, content to read books, play the piano or listen to music on the family stereo. She developed a special affinity for Mozart, in part because she thought Wolfgang was such a fascinating name, but also because his light, lilting melodies enchanted her and stimulated her already active imagination. Her mother naturally encouraged this, accepting that Julie was not experiencing a typical childhood, and did not wish to stunt her artistic growth. Julie also loved singing and had a sweet, engaging voice. Before Julie reached the age of four, Anne Creighton was no longer able to accurately count the number of songs her progeny retained in her ever increasing repertoire.

Anne found it both exciting and unsettling that her daughter was a gifted and unusual child. Julie did not behave in a manner consistent with her age, often living in a world of her own, filled with music, books, and her vivid imagination. Although she enjoyed playing with other children, it was not something she actively sought. In fact, when other children excluded her from their activities, Julie did not even seem to be aware of it. Anne worried that Julie would be hurt by the rejection of the neighborhood children. Her concern, however, was abated by the undeniable fact that Julie was a happy and agreeable child, and either did not notice, or did not care that she was different from the other children.

Unlike many children who exhibit jealousy at the birth of a younger sibling, Anne was pleased that Julie seemed thrilled with her new brother and proud to be her mother's helper, feeding, fetching diapers, and her favorite job of all, singing her baby brother lullabies until he was asleep. The peaceful little boy quickly grew accustomed to his big sister singing him to sleep, and in fact, became dependent upon it. The bond between brother and sister was clear and unbreakable. Dr. and Mrs. Creighton breathed a sigh of relief that their two children loved each other with such devotion. It certainly made parenting easier.

The Creighton children led an idyllic existence, brought up in a comfortable home with love, laughter and music. Spats between the siblings were rare and minor. Their parents doted on them, and John Creighton was especially proud when little Philip showed an interest in becoming a surgeon, just like his Daddy. They were thankful for the blessing of a close, happy family. Life couldn't be better.

4

As Julie fought back the sadness which threatened to engulf her every time she saw the Jaguar, she turned, quietly entered the house, and carefully set her cello down in the music room. Predictably, the house came alive with activity once her presence was detected. Johann and Sebastienne tore through the upstairs hallway, down the banister, bounding through the downstairs rooms full tilt toward Julie, somersaulting and falling over each other gracelessly and having at last reached her, resumed the detached air of the cats she had rescued and loved since they were small enough to fit in the palms of her hands. Not far behind them was Fred, trailing an endless supply of dog hair which floated through the air, settling on carpet, furniture and anything else in its path. Julie loved her pets, and it was their love for her and their perceptiveness to her emotional turmoil that aided her in accepting and facing Jack's untimely death.

Rather than behaving like the self-centered, attention-demanding animals consistent with their nature, they were attentive and sensitive to Julie's grief, quietly loving her, petting her with their paws and noses. Telling her the best they knew how, that everything was going to be all right; that whatever she was so sad about, they were there for her and always would be.

Spats between the pets stopped altogether as they worried and fussed over Julie. On many occasions, Julie had thrown her arms around Fred, the huge German Shepherd, and cried, her face buried in his thick fur; or held the cats tightly to her chest, stroking them while she sobbed. They would tenderly lick her tears away and nuzzle her, absorbing her sorrow. Eventually, the animals seemed to understand Jack was not returning, and went through their own period of mourning.

Cats and dog were only too happy when Julie's life returned to something more normal, even if it did take her away from them. Now, they were welcoming her home as if she had been gone for weeks instead of hours.

After cooing and fussing over them and giving everyone their due in tummy rubs and ear scratches, Julie took Fred out for his afternoon constitutional. With sixty-two acres at his disposal, he was in doggie heaven, chasing, but never catching rabbits, squirrels and anything else smart enough to run from him. When he finished doing all the important things dogs have to do, he ran back to Julie, panting and ready to go back inside, something Julie was getting impatient to do as well.

Although not still in deep grief, she found herself often restless and sometimes edgy. Dog and mistress went inside through the kitchen door, and all animals were given their dinner and fresh water. Julie loved caring for them even more since Jack's death, and their perceptiveness to her grief further strengthened the bond between animal and human.

5

Julie was especially grateful for the companionship of her pets now that Su Li would be gone for weeks, perhaps even three or four months. Su Li had received an upsetting phone call from her brother, informing her that their mother was critically ill. Julie felt sick at heart to hear of Miyso's condition, and sadly helped Su Li prepare for her trip to California. The house was empty without her to fuss, cook, clean, and provide the cheerful and devoted friendship that she and Su Li had spent a lifetime cultivating.

Su Li's family was one of the first of a wave of Vietnamese refugees to arrive in St. Louis in the early 1980's. They lost everything but their lives in order to come to America, arriving with only the clothes they were wearing. Industrious, hardworking, and once proud, they asked for no handouts, only the required sponsorship from an American family and an opportunity to work and be productive.

Julie's generous and philanthropic parents were moved with compassion, her mother openly weeping at the heartrending pictures invading their affluent home on the evening news, and soon applied to sponsor a family. Dr. and Mrs. Creighton opened their hearts, their home, and their pocketbooks to Su Li who was four at the time, her baby brother, Wanh, fifteen months, and their parents, Miyso and Tan. The Tuans were one of the fortunate few whose family left Vietnam and reached the United States intact. They arrived with a host of medical problems and nutritional deficiencies, which fortunately Julie's father could expertly treat. Mr. Tuan had a better than average grasp of the English language, but his wife knew only rudimentary phrases. They also brought with them a humble gratitude which would last a lifetime.

"House like fairy tale," Tan whispered when the family arrived.

"You and the baby will be in the guest room, here," Anne said, as she led them down a wide hallway. "Su Li will share a room with our daughter, Julie."

"T'ank you."

"Julie is very excited to have a new friend and little sister."

"Yes. T'ank you," replied Tan, while Miyso nodded in agreement. The Tuans did their best with the English they knew, and a bond of friendship quickly formed that crossed cultural and language barriers.

Su Li's mother, Miyso Tuan, immediately assumed the role of housekeeper in the Creighton home, a position that was neither asked, nor expected of her. Anne was surprised at how quickly the two families from different cultures and parts of the world became friends. She tried in vain to explain to Miyso that she didn't expect service from her. The Creighton home was large enough to accommodate two families with plenty of room to spare, and she had a maid, but Anne was incapable of fully comprehending the horrors this family witnessed on a daily basis, nor their need to express thankfulness to these hospitable strangers. Death on a grand scale, atrocities that could not be spoken of, forever leached into the memory of this tiny woman to whom fear and terror were constant companions. Her face was lined beyond her years, her forlorn eyes having seen more than the human psyche was intended to discern. Anne did not understand that Miyso would have done anything to be in America with her husband and children, or that she viewed her service to the Creightons as nothing more than a small gesture of appreciation.

Julie was ten when the Tuans came to live with them. Their first meeting was exciting and unforgettable. Little Su Li was fascinated with Julie's long red hair which hung naturally in spiral curls, and would have played with it endlessly had Miyso not sharply reprimanded her in a quick, staccato tongue. Julie was equally enthralled with Su Li and her silky, black hair, which was bone straight. She seemed like a tiny, beautiful doll to Julie, her almond eyes set in pale golden skin, her frame small and dainty, a cherubic smile on her sweet, round face. Only she was not a delicate toy; she was alive. Julie's shyness vanished when she was around Su Li, despite a six year age difference. The girls became fast friends, and Anne Creighton was the one who ended up being grateful the Tuans had come to live with them for reasons Miyso would never understand.

Julie now had a rapt audience when she played the piano. Su Li was not only her faithful friend and constant shadow; she was the biggest and only member of the Juliette Creighton Fan Club. When Julie was in school, Su Li missed her terribly, but used the time as an opportunity to work on her English, tutored by her father when he was not working in the hospital cafeteria. She also learned homemaking skills from her mother, who never wanted the Creightons to see her family as a burden.

In the fourth grade, Julie's school provided the opportunity for interested students to take instrumental music classes. For the fourth graders, this meant stringed instruments only; woodwinds, reeds, brass and percussion were not offered until the sixth grade. Excitedly, she brought the permission slip home for her parents' signatures. She was certain that once she got her violin home, Mozart's *Eine Kleine Nachtmusik* would be hers. Her mother knew differently. No matter how talented Julie was, a violin still had to be mastered, and the last thing Anne Creighton wanted to subject her back teeth fillings to, was a ten year old child screeching on a beginner's violin.

"Can I get a violin? Please, Mom, please? It'll be so great! Can I get a violin, huh, Mom, please?"

"No, Julie, not a violin," her mother answered, thinking bagpipes would be preferable to a violin.

"Please, Mom? I won't ask for anything else. Not ever. Not for Christmas, not for my birthday, not for playing well at my piano recitals. Oh, Mom! Now, I can have violin recitals! Just think how much you would love to hear me play at my violin recitals! Can I get a violin, huh? *Pleeeeease!* I'll clean my room every day. Just think, Mom, after I practice my piano lessons, I can practice on my violin!"

Her mother *was* thinking. She was thinking of ingesting large doses of migraine medication in the immediate future. She needed to extricate herself from this situation soon, and at the moment nothing was coming to mind. "No, Julie, no violin," was the only answer Anne could think of. Her day had been busy, and she was too tired to think clearly, a fact Julie was ignoring.

"Just think, Mom, *Eine Kleine Nachtmusik*! I bet the teacher lets me play it just like on the record. I really, really want a violin, Mom. I just *have* to have a violin! Please say, yes. I'll be so good forever."

"No, Julie, not a violin." Anne was hoping Julie could not detect the tiredness in her voice, but Julie could give a woodpecker a headache.

Julie was undaunted. "I know I can play it just beautifully. Besides, when I'm all grown up and play with the symphony, it'll be easier to get a job. They only have one pianist, but Mom, did you ever see how many violinists there are when we go to Powell Hall? Tons of violinists, every time we go, Mom, just tons, and I can be one of them in case I don't get a job playing piano. Please can I get a violin?"

"How about a cello, Julie?"

"Okay!"

Su Li's father, Tan was integrating well in his new country and eventually met other refugees who were farther along socially and economically than he was. They had business opportunities they wanted to discuss with him that if successful, would allow him and his family to soon be independent. The Tuans were grateful for the help the Creightons had provided, but wanted to be out on their own in their new country. Tan was already a licensed driver and no longer needed John Creighton to drive him to his job at the hospital cafeteria. The Tuans had made a few friends, mostly other refugee families, and Mr. Tuan was on his way to a meeting with these men, excited about his promising future when he was hit broadside by a drunk driver and killed.

Miyso accepted the news of Tan's death with a dignity she did not feel. She had survived the horrific inhumanities of Vietnam and lived to see her family arrive together in this new land of opportunity, in spite of every conceivable hardship. She never imagined that once they were safe, in a beautiful city such as Ladue, of all places, she would be without her husband as a result of someone else's foolish choice. The Tuans harbored hope after their dramatic escape from Vietnam, that in their new land, all such violence had been left behind.

Behind her stoic façade, Miyso's heart wretched in sorrow. Her command of the English language was halting and she was lost without her husband.

The original plan for sponsorship intended for sponsored families and individuals to be self-supporting and independent after learning the language and obtaining job skills. Unsure of what her future now held, Miyso approached Anne for advice. She was concerned that she had nothing to offer and was afraid of being turned out. But Anne assured her, her fears were for naught.

Miyso accepted friendship and heartfelt sympathy from the Creightons, who repeatedly assured her that she and the children were welcome in their home for as long as they needed. Miyso was in a nearly impossible predicament. But what she never knew was that although their hearts ached with hers, John and

Anne's reasons for asking her to remain were, in fact, selfish. Su Li had such a normalizing effect on Julie, they were afraid Julie would be devastated or perhaps retreat into her own world if Su Li left.

Miyso and the children remained in the Creighton home, but she vowed to master her new language and recommitted herself to not being a burden.

Julie put her arms around Su Li and hugged her tightly. It had to be worse than awful to have your Daddy killed. She told her she would share her own Daddy with Su Li and the baby. She was sure Philip wouldn't mind sharing either. She hoped her own Daddy would never be killed by a drunk driver.

Julie had her school cello now and brought it home daily so she could work on this wonderful new instrument. Su Li sat spellbound, listening to Julie practice. As always, Julie, who was normally shy, reveled in the presence of an appreciative audience. Su Li did not exactly possess a discriminating ear.

"We just have to do pizzicato 'til the teacher tells us we can use the bow," Julie solemnly informed Su Li one evening.

"What's a pizzicato?" Su Li asked, wide-eyed to be privy to this new information.

"It's when you pluck the strings with your right hand to make the sound. Like this." She demonstrated with flair. "The first week we could only do open strings, but now we can put our fingers on the fingerboard to make more notes." She displayed the full extent of her new ability, which she managed to convince Su Li was vast.

"That's so pretty, Julie," Su Li gasped.

"Yes, I know, thank you." Julie was trying to remember her manners, but she still had not told Su Li what she was planning to do. "I do have the bow in my cello case, you know," she continued, with dramatic panache.

Su Li gasped again. "But you're not s'posed to use it 'til the teacher says!"

"But the teacher isn't here, and Instrumental Music isn't 'til all the way to Monday and this is only Thursday, and I am ready to move ahead. Mom has a record of this guy named Pablo Casals, and he plays the cello, only he uses the bow, and know what Su Li? It's the most beautiful music you ever heard. It touches my heart and tingles my ears, and makes me all goose-pimply to hear it. Besides, I heard Mom and Daddy talking when they thought I was asleep and they said I was a musical genius, so I figure I can use the bow. I'm sure I will sound like Pablo Casals very soon."

"I'm sure, too," Su Li replied, nodding her head, her eyes wide with admiration. Julie was certain that Su Li had no idea what a musical genius even was. For that matter, neither did Julie, but it sounded important. However, she was satisfied her words had left Su Li awe struck to be in Julie's presence. Julie relished having a fan club, even if the membership consisted of only one.

Julie removed the bow from its protective pouch, and to her profound disappointment, discovered the horsehair was too slack to produce any music at all when she drew it across the strings.

"Something's wrong with this bow. The white stringy stuff is all loose. It won't make the right sound. The bow is supposed to be tighter. I know. We have season tickets to the symphony and I'm going to play cello there for my job when I grow up. I know these things, you know," she informed Su Li with absolute certainty.

Julie had Su Li convinced that Julie knew everything. She left no room for Su Li to doubt a word Julie uttered. "What are you gonna do?" Su Li asked eagerly.

"Easy. Fix it."

"How?"

"Not sure yet. Gotta check this thing out." She examined the bow carefully, trying to figure out how to tighten the horsehair. "Hey! This screw thing on the bottom moves. I bet if I just keep twisting…"

Su Li inhaled so much air so suddenly, Julie thought her friend might be choking to death, but when she looked up at her friend, all she saw was a horrified look on Su Li's face.

"Whatever's the matt…Uh-oh." All of the horsehair was hanging loose at the frog, which had separated from the bottom of the bow. Mortified, Julie could not admit to her most ardent admirer that she had no idea of what to do next, nor did she have a clue as to what she had just managed to do to her school bow. She knew she was in trouble with the teacher, and probably her parents as well if they found out, but her most desperate and immediate need was to save face in front of Su Li.

"Yes, this is what I thought was wrong," she stated confidently, holding the screw in her hand. "This bow was broken when I got it and will need to be replaced, as you can see by the way it fell apart."

Su Li nodded in complete agreement.

When a penitent Julie showed the teacher the bow Monday morning, she was firmly reprimanded. The frog had only to be reconnected, but the teacher, Miss Marshall, was perplexed that of all the students in instrumental music, Julie Creighton had been the one to disobey. She was Miss Marshall's best pupil. Not only that, she was painfully shy, timid and always well-behaved.

Julie squirmed as Miss Marshall questioned her as to whether Julie was covering up for one of her friends. Julie's eyes welled with tears, and Miss Marshall ceased pressing this extremely sensitive child further. It would be unforgiveable to traumatize a student. Julie's enthusiasm for music should be encouraged, not hindered. Julie's innate ability could never belie the artistic temperament which made itself known to Miss Marshall as early as the first day of class.

Julie sensed that Miss Marshall was aggravated at her for ignoring her instructions and was afraid of what her consequences would be. As if the situation wasn't bad enough, the principal was patrolling the halls and when she saw Miss Marshall speaking to Julie, entered her classroom and looked sternly at the bow. To Julie's surprise, Miss Marshall informed the principal, who knew nothing about instruments, that the bow in question was faulty and there was no need to contact the Creightons, as Julie had done nothing wrong.

Julie was unsure why she was not in more trouble than she had originally feared. She did not understand why her teacher had protected her. But she vowed to listen more carefully to Miss Marshall, whom she genuinely liked. She felt sad when Miss Marshall told her how disappointed she was that the bow had been tampered with before the class was instructed in its proper use. Julie would try to listen better. Instrumental music was her favorite class, but she still didn't like being held back by less talented classmates.

Over the next eight years, with Miyso, Su Li and Wanh living with the Creightons, the bond between Su Li and Julie had cemented, and when Julie left after graduation to study at the Peabody Conservatory in Baltimore, both girls felt empty, deeply missing each other. Their lives had been so interwoven, their friendship so close, that it seemed as if each of them were missing a piece of themselves. But during school breaks, Julie always came home, and it was as if nothing had changed.

Six years later, when Su Li graduated from high school, she left Ladue to live with Julie, who by that time had successfully auditioned for a cellist position that was open with the Columbus Symphony. She cooked and kept house for Julie, just as her mother had done for Anne. Miyso and Wanh moved to California, determined to make it on their own, knowing that if Wanh continued to excel in his studies, he had a chance of going to college on an academic scholarship. He had a perfect 4.0 average and was in all honor classes. Julie tried to interest Su Li in furthering her education, but Su Li, ever faithful to her dearest friend, was determined to remain with Julie, whom she was convinced could not live without her.

Julie never learned to cook, was, in fact, quite terrible at it, and as long as she could find what she needed, never spent much time doing housework. Su Li, however, was skilled in both culinary and home management skills and loved being in the apartment taking care of the more practical matters of home life, while listening to her friend practice. She was devoted to Julie, and Julie silently vowed she would never take that for granted.

Julie's dream since childhood was to play with the St. Louis Symphony Orchestra. She had always imagined she would walk into Powell Hall, audition, and awe-struck by her ability, the committee would hire her immediately as the symphony's new cellist. Before her first semester break at Peabody, however, Julie got her first dose of reality.

Competition in her choice of life's work was fierce and even though she was gifted beyond most, she pushed herself to practice no less than eight hours a day, usually ten to twelve. Throughout her years in grade school and high school, music had been easy for Julie. Her ability was far above anyone else's in music class, and for that matter, above the students which her private teachers had as well. At the conservatory, however, Julie was only one of many immensely talented and able students. Hard work as she had never known, relentless dedication, and a little luck would be the only factors that would separate those students who would go on to have performing jobs from those who would eventually seek other careers, or simply teach music. But Julie wanted to perform in a symphony, particularly the St. Louis Symphony Orchestra. Everything else in her life would be sacrificed on the altar of self-denial so her dream could become reality.

During her final year of studies, she joined a discussion group in the student union hall.

"You have to join the American Federation of Musicians if you intend to get anywhere in your career," one of the bassoon players was opining.

"What's the American Federation of Musicians and why do we have to join it?" Julie asked.

"One of the big draws, among other things, is that you will receive the monthly publication, *The International Musician*. This publication advertises the symphonies that have openings and are holding auditions. It's your best chance to achieve the goals you have worked so hard for around here."

A trombonist horned in, "Yeah, but you need to also keep your ears open and meet as many people as you can. That can also increase your chances of hearing through the grapevine of positions that might be open anywhere."

A flautist piped up, "Thanks. We need all the help we can get!"

An oboist whined, "But the job market is so tough out there. This is *so* much work, and what if it's all for nothing?"

But the percussionist hammered the oboist. "If you didn't want to work, then what are you doing here? The symphonies take the best of the best. If you can't take the heat, get out of the kitchen."

The pianist in the group soft pedaled her response. "We need to do all of these things. Plus, we need a little luck along the way.

Plenty of good musicians never realize their dream in spite of their best efforts."

A high-strung violinist snapped, "I can't take it anymore. The stress!"

Julie took their advice to heart. Eventually her perseverance paid off. After auditioning in Atlanta, Miami, and Cleveland and not being hired, she arrived in Columbus and played extremely well, advancing to the finals and beating out over one hundred cellists, obtaining fifth seating. Julie knew no one in Columbus except Su Li of course, but she was now playing in a professional orchestra and being paid for it.

On her own in a strange city, Julie was uncomfortable and retreated into her music. Although it was not necessary for her to practice more than four hours a day unless the music was particularly difficult, Julie practiced for eight, lost in her own world, trying to adjust to her new life. Su Li fretted over her, but by now she knew that immersing herself in her work was Julie's way of coping and in the end, she would be even better for all the practicing.

"Hey Julie," Su Li asked, "Would you like to learn to cook something easy?"

"Why?" Julie responded, as though she had never heard such an outrageous suggestion.

"For one thing, cooking is fun. And there is a sense of accomplishment when you create a satisfying meal."

"Music is fun," Julie replied. "And there is also a sense of accomplishment when you play a cello solo you have worked on for weeks that reaches into the hearts of thousands."

"What are you going to do if I ever marry someone and move away? How do you plan to eat if you never learn to cook?"

"Are you even dating anybody?"

"Okay, no."

"Are you even interested in anybody?"

"Not yet."

"Then I guess I'll worry about that when it happens."

After more than a year passed, Julie heard rumors that the St. Louis Symphony Orchestra would be auditioning for one seat in the cello section. Immediately Julie wrote, sending in her resume and requesting a list of the excerpts and pieces required for the audition. By the time the ad appeared in *The International Musician*, she had already purchased the necessary music and was preparing an audition tape.

Arriving at Lambert International Airport, Julie smiled to herself. This was the first audition for which her travel would not incur any hotel or food expenses. She was going home. Her parents met her at the airport with great fanfare and soon she was back in her childhood bedroom in Ladue.

The next morning she stepped into Powell Hall. Every warm, wonderful memory raced through her mind, flooding her with nostalgia. As a child, The Hall enthralled her; she had imagined it a castle, with its plush red seats and draperies, the ivory walls trimmed in gold, the grand staircase covered in rich, red carpeting, the domed ceiling and the ornate embellishments had left her breathless with delight. Everything was red, gold and ivory, and at Christmas time, it was decorated more beautifully than even Santa's place at the North Pole, she had been sure of that. Elegantly decorated trees and wreaths graced every level, and boughs of greenery hung from the balconies announcing the season of peace and good will. The sound of Handel's *Messiah* would fill the hearts of all who heard it with reverence and peace. Tears filled her eyes and a lump formed in her throat to be back home in the place she desperately longed to work, knowing her chances of doing so were slim. She was lucky to have a job at all, and Columbus was not a bad symphony in the least. It just wasn't home.

Although Julie was more prepared for this audition than she had ever been prepared for anything in her life, nerves gripped her stomach like a vise. It was do or die. This was where she had always dreamed of playing, her ultimate goal in life. She always did her best at other auditions because she wanted and needed a job, but to play at Powell Hall was to come home, and this would most likely be her only opportunity, possibly, in her entire career. An opening for a cellist in a symphony of this caliber was rare. To make matters worse, she discovered there were nearly two hundred other hopeful cellists vying for that one coveted position. Her audition time was 10:30 a.m., and she was early. She paced the floor, waiting to be called.

At last it was her turn. When it was all over, she felt as if she had been cheated, not allowed to strut her best stuff, and she left feeling deflated and defeated. She called Su Li, who answered on the first ring.

"Well? How'd it go?"

"I'm so upset."

"What happened?"

"There were 38 measures from *The Marriage of Figaro Overture* by Mozart, 20 measures from a Brahms Symphony, a slow movement of Beethoven's *Symphony in C Minor*, slow movement from *Number 5*, a few measures from Mendelssohn's *A Midsummer Night's Dream* and 40 measures from a Haydn cello concerto."

"Okay. That sounds about par for the course. Why are you upset?"

"All in all, my turn in the spotlight was less than 15 minutes."

"Julie, that's all it ever is on these auditions."

"But this is Powell Hall, Su Li. This is *home*."

"When will you hear?"

"Hopefully, this afternoon. I don't see how they can tell anything from these little snippets of sound."

"Call me when you know something."

By 4:00 that afternoon she was notified that she had advanced to the semi-finals and was expected back the following afternoon. Her confidence somewhat restored, Julie returned to The Hall and was asked to play her solo piece, followed by some sight reading. Again, it went by too quickly for Julie to feel satisfied.

She called Su Li.

"I played well, but we won't know if I advance to the finals for at least a month. I'll be home tonight."

"At least you have a busy concert schedule here in Columbus, so it will help the time go faster. You won't even have time to think of the finals in St. Louis."

"Yeah, we also have a recording session. Lots to do. I hope I hear soon. It's killing me to pay full price for airfare, but I never know how long I will be staying. Plus, I've had to take time off work for the audition and hopefully, for the finals. I'm going to have to make up my losses."

"You could ask your father for help," Su Li offered, but she knew that by now Julie was fiercely independent and she would rather chew glass than ask for help.

"I figure it won't be too long before I'm making enough money to put a dent in some of the debt I've accumulated as a result of choosing the life of a musician."

"Like there was another life you could have been happy living? You could never be this passionate about any other life. You were born to play music, Julie. Quit whining."

Six weeks later, Julie received a letter in the mail notifying her that she had indeed advanced to the finals. In three weeks she was to return to St. Louis. "Su Li, if I get this job, I'll never move again!"

"Unless they fire you," Su Li teased.

"I'm laughing hysterically. Somebody stop me," Julie replied, unamused. "Well," she sighed, "I guess this will max out my credit card, but if I make this audition, it will be worth everything. In addition to being home, the pay in St. Louis is better and the cost of living is cheaper. Please God, this is all I want."

"He's heard that line before, you know."

"But this time I mean it. Su Li, this is everything I have ever wanted. Since I was a little girl. What are the chances that there was an opening at this time in my life? I'm not married and I'm not even dating anybody. So there are no personal conflicts, no ties to this city, everything is perfect to move back home. Oh, Su Li, I want this more than anything!"

"Johann and Sebastienne are not going to like moving," Su Li reminded her.

"They'll never have to do it again. I'll even buy them caviar when we get settled. This will be the toughest part of the competition. I haven't even heard the others. Maybe that's for the best."

"Good luck, Julie. Promise you'll call me when you finish your final audition."

"You know I will." It would be up to Su Li to calm Julie's nerves and help her put her life back in perspective. She had watched in frustrated silence as Julie made the semi-finals in Atlanta and the finals in Miami only to be rejected as she had been in Cleveland. To come this far and not be chosen in St. Louis could be the worst thing to happen in Julie's life, but the reality was that there was only one opening to be filled by only one person, and Julie was one of many yet to go to finals.

Julie flew back to St. Louis for the last part of the most important audition of her life.

"How'd it go, Julie?" Su Li carefully questioned her friend over the telephone.

"I was nervous, of course, but I didn't make any mistakes. I wish I could go back and do it again. I know I could do better. I was tired and strained. I wish I could have just seen this as another audition in another city for another symphony, but I couldn't. I want this position more than anything, and I just don't know, Su Li. I just don't know." Julie sounded edgy, high strung and disappointed in herself. Su Li recognized the familiar tension in Julie's voice, and knowing her as she did, envisioned Julie pacing back and forth, running her fingers through her hair. She had watched this same scenario played out in all of Julie's previous auditions.

Su Li knew there was no way to placate Julie. To attempt to do so would be condescending at best, infuriating at worst. "When are you coming back to Columbus?"

"I should be in at eleven tomorrow morning. Mother and Daddy are taking me to the oh-so-very-swank Tony's downtown for dinner tonight and out again for breakfast in the morning. Mother says I'm too thin and Daddy says I'm not eating properly and will end up with a nutritional deficiency, so they're making sure they do their part to keep me alive and well. In other words, my parents are fine."

"I'll see you at the airport, Julie. Try to relax. What's done is done. You might as well force yourself to enjoy a meal at a five star restaurant. It's a real sacrifice, but I'm glad you're willing to make it. As for me, I am heating up a delicious frozen pizza for my supper. My mouth is watering already from anticipation. Do your best to enjoy Tony's and try not to think of me savoring my frozen pizza. It will only make you feel deprived." They rang off and Julie, feeling better, got ready for dinner.

Two months passed before Julie received the news that the opening for Violoncellist with the St. Louis Symphony Orchestra would be filled by none other than Juliette Glynne Creighton.

Within two months, Julie, Su Li, and the cats had settled into a condo in the city's fashionable Central West End, Julie happier than she had been in her entire life. Now, with her life in order, maybe she could feel normal, whatever that meant.

6

Julie was unusually tired, having been off of work for several months of funeral leave. She wished she had not taken such a long leave. On one hand, she was numb for what seemed like an eternity, and believed she was in no condition to perform and take on the grueling schedule of practice, rehearsal, and performance. On the other hand, having been out for so long, her first day back was exhausting. Having to deal with several of the other members welcoming her back, expressing their sympathy, had taken an emotional toll on her. She was shy to begin with, and uncomfortable dealing with well-meaning people. All she wanted to do was rehearse as planned and go home. And then there was the added stress of the bizarre episode with the guy in the Buick.

She had promised Su Li she would eat regularly, but it was too tempting to skip dinner and go to bed, despite the early hour. She poured a glass of port and to her pets' delight, headed upstairs to sleep while it was still light outside.

The next morning, Julie ran errands. Still unnerved from having been followed, she made a special point to be aware of her surroundings. She wanted to be sure that yesterday's stalking incident did not happen again.

She arrived safely home, grateful there were no scheduled rehearsals today. She played outside with Fred and her stress melted away. He was a good catharsis for whatever ailed her. They finally went inside for food and water.

Julie walked into the hearth room to check the answering machine, more out of habit than actually expecting to find anybody wanting to speak with her. She knew that if there was no message from Su Li, she would hear from her tonight. Miyso was consumed with cancer and Su Li was now in California to spend time with her mother for whatever amount of time she had left, probably not more than a few months, maybe even weeks.

Miyso's tiny body was withered and racked with pain. Julie was distressed to hear of Miyso's suffering; she had been like a second mother to her. It seemed to Julie that Miyso's entire life had been spent in pain and suffering. She wondered if any of the short years she and Wanh had spent in California held any happiness for her. She wept silently, thinking of Miyso and of Su Li, and the grief that lay ahead for her sweet friend.

She had given Su Li several thousand dollars for her trip to California, with express instructions to let her know if more was needed. Jack Davenport had left his widow very well provided for and no amount of money was too great if any of the Tuan family were in need.

The answering machine whirred on and revealed two hang-ups and a reminder call from Julie's dentist for her semi-annual appointment. After a long silence on the fourth call, a man's gravelly voice broke in. "Confession is good for the soul." He sounded threatening.

Julie, taken aback at first, stifled a nervous giggle. "Okay. I confess. I lusted after the new oboe player in rehearsal yesterday. I couldn't help it. He was really cute. Get a life." She dismissed the creep as having nothing better to do on a lovely day.

Julie thought what an odd day yesterday had been and today was becoming. First, Su Li left, and then there was the car that followed her, now this bizarre phone call. Living out in the woods with an unlisted number, crank calls were rare. Jack was usually the one to answer the phone and if needed, could be counted on to supply a quick answer to the occasional prankster.

Her machine had no sooner rewound, than the telephone rang. Julie picked it up on the first ring, hoping to hear from Su Li, and was unsettled to hear the voice of the same man. "Confession is good for your soul, Julie," he whispered, barely audible. "Isn't there something you want to say, Julie?"

"Who is this? What do you want?" she demanded angrily. Immediately, she realized he used her name, and she involuntarily shuddered as she felt a chill snaking up her spine. He had spoken her name. This was no ordinary crank call—this was personal. She began to feel light headed and breathed deeply.

"I want to know what you have done with it." His voice darkened the room. "Where is it? Think about it, Julie. It's in your best interest to be a good girl."

She slammed the phone down, shaken. She felt the blood draining from her face and her legs became watery. Who was he, and how did he know her name? She swallowed hard, placing her hand on the phone table for support. Her hand was shaking. She did not recognize his voice, but knew she could identify it if she heard it again. It was low, throaty, menacing. *He should switch to filtered cigarettes.* She laughed at her own joke in an attempt to regain her composure.

Julie was alone in the house. Jack was dead and Su Li was in California. At least she had Fred. Jack had always seemed concerned for Julie's safety and Fred was trained to protect her, but she was still rattled and unnerved by this last call.

There was only one thing to do. Julie kept a hidden safe tucked behind her favorite Monet print on the wall of the hearth room. From it, she removed a gold box. Inside the gold box was Julie's answer to stress, depression, anxiety and loneliness. This was a gift from Jack, saved for whenever the need was greatest and secreted away in a temperature controlled wall safe. She sat down in Jack's overstuffed recliner, leaned back and opened the box.

Because the past two days had been exceptionally lonely and stressful, Julie picked out one of her favorites. It was a scalloped shaped, milk chocolate filled with a hazelnut ganache. These chocolates, imported from Belgium, were the finest in the world. Julie, being very serious about her chocolate, had endeavored to taste the best that Switzerland, France, and the United States had to offer, but as gratifying as those had been, nothing, absolutely nothing could compare with these Belgian chocolates. Jack had a standing order for them to be shipped once a year on Valentine's Day to Julie. It was up to her to see that they lasted as long as possible.

She picked up her chosen piece, tenderly removing it from the holder, leaned her head back, and closing her eyes, placed the chocolate in her mouth. The decadent masterpiece slowly began to permeate her mouth, the chocolate silk coating her teeth and tongue, its rich, buttery smoothness filling her senses with creamy goodness. The hazelnut cream filling, rich, nutty, and slightly sweet, blended in comforting perfection with the luxuriant chocolate that encased it. Chocolate and hazelnut flavors were a perfect complement when combined in the mouth and this delectable delicacy united the finest of both. The roof of her mouth was gilded in chocolate satin as the chocolate began to melt and merge within her, taking her away, a willing captive to its luscious charm. She relaxed, as stress and tension drifted far away, drowned in a river of chocolate enchantment. She was soon lost in a world of plush, chocolate velvet...

He appeared in the room with her. She rose to meet him, a lump in her throat. He held out his arms to receive her and she held him tightly, her face buried in his chest.

"They told me you were dead," she whispered.

"You shouldn't believe everything you hear. I would never leave you, Juliette. I could never leave you. You're the only woman I've ever loved." He was smiling at her, his sapphire eyes sparkling down at her, so handsome beneath his black hair. He ran his fingers through her thick red hair and she closed her eyes, absorbing his sensations.

He was kissing her now, her face cupped in one hand, his other hand massaging the nape of her neck, gently but firmly working its way slowly down her back, rotating in small circles, as his lips moved down her neck, inch by inch, lower and lower, his breathing matching hers as she trembled at his touch. His hands were caressing her, squeezing her just as they had on their honeymoon, and she felt faint.

"Oh Jack."

The ringing of the telephone startled her back to the present and she rose to answer it, the last of the chocolate fading to a pleasant memory.

"Hello?"

"Give me what I want, or I'll come and get it for myself, Julie," threatened the voice.

"Leave me alone you creep."

"Remember, Julie, confession is good for the soul."

"I don't know what you're talking about. Stop calling me!" She slammed the phone down, pressing her shaking hand over her heart, beating rapidly with fear as she struggled for control. *Breathe. Just breathe.*

She wished Su Li hadn't left. She knew she would be calling soon, but she couldn't tell her about this, not with the burden Su Li was already bearing. Julie was definitely shaken now. She wished she wasn't alone. She picked up the phone and dialed her good friend and closest neighbor.

"Hey, Meg, want to come over for dinner?" Julie forced herself to sound normal.

"I thought Su Li left this morning."

"She left yesterday morning."

"Who's cooking?" Meg sounded curious.

"I am. Why don't you come on over?"

"No way. I have this goal in life, to live at least 'til tomorrow. You could burn salad. I'll come if you promise to order pizza."

"Oh, come on. I'm not *that* bad."

"Julie," Meg continued slowly, emphasizing each word as if she were talking to a child. "Assuming you can even find the kitchen, you have no idea what it's there for. You don't even *begin* to know what people do in a kitchen."

"Stop picking on me. Su Li left plenty of food. She told me before she left that the kitchen was very well stocked. You know how thorough she is, and how she fusses."

"What is the kitchen stocked with, Julie?"

"I don't know yet, I haven't checked."

"Hah! I knew it! You haven't even been in there yet! You are totally clueless as to what Su Li even left for you, yet you expect me to come and eat your cooking. What have you got against me, anyway?"

"Magdalene Curtis."

"Don't call me that!"

"Magdalene, Magdalene, Magdalene."

"Okay, I'm coming."

"That's better."

"You'll do anything to get your way."

"I know. I'm ruthless. Besides, I need to talk to you."

"Good. We can talk. That way, I won't have to eat." She hung up before Julie could reply, but at least she was on her way over and that made Julie feel safer. Meg would know what to do.

Julie and Meg had forged an unlikely friendship. Julie's best friend in the world was Su Li. Her other friends and acquaintances had all been debutantes, musicians, and people from backgrounds similar to Julie's. John and Anne would not have thought highly of Meg. Su Li considered her crass and coarse at best, not in the same league as Julie, who was refined and possessed the effortless elegance that came naturally to a lady raised with class and every advantage as Julie had been. Su Li didn't like Meg; she had said she was an ill-suited friend for Julie, but knew it was pointless to make an issue of it with Julie. Su Li had spoken her peace on the issue, and with the wisdom achieved through years of friendship, remained silent on the subject after that, unwilling to engage in an exercise of futility.

Meg was Julie's age, twice divorced and lived in a rundown trailer on a small piece of land a few acres in back of the Davenport property. Jack had met her one day while exploring an old logging road he discovered when taking Fred for a walk.

He invited her over to meet his new bride. Meg was the closest thing Julie had to a next door neighbor, being some sixty-plus acres away. By cutting over the logging trail on foot, she could be at Julie's house faster than if she took her car around the hills and passes on the main road.

Meg was the seventh of nine unwanted children born to an alcoholic father and a mother who dropped out of high school when she was pregnant with Meg's oldest brother. She grew up poor and she grew up fast. While the advantages of privilege came naturally for Julie, Meg and her siblings learned to survive without basic necessities. Meg was tough and street smart and the contrast between her and Julie was stark.

Julie found Meg refreshing and honest. Meg was down to earth and said whatever she felt like saying, whenever she felt like saying it. Julie would always battle shyness whenever she was away from her music, her animals, and Su Li. She believed Meg helped to broaden her world and bring her out of her shell. She thought Su Li was overprotective and possibly even jealous because Julie had room in her life for another friend. But Julie believed Su Li acted in her best interest, in spite of their disagreement over the unconventional friendship.

Meg seemed at ease in Julie's elegant home, but each time they visited, it was always at Julie's. She was never invited to Meg's trailer, had never even seen it, Julie assumed, because Meg was embarrassed. It made no difference to Julie. She enjoyed Meg's friendship wherever it took place. Meg and Jack had gotten along well; Julie only wished that Su Li would warm up to her, too.

While she waited for Meg to arrive, Julie checked the doors and windows of the house and satisfied all was secured, she hugged her big dog who padded around, following her from room to room.

"You're such a good boy, Fred. You gonna keep Mommy safe from that nasty old man that keeps calling, aren't you, sweetie-pie," she cooed to him.

He wagged his tail and pushed his head into her hand, assuring her he would always be there for her. As she bent down to hug him again, Fred growled and raised his hackles. Tearing away from her, he ran to the kitchen door, but started wagging his tail at the sight of Meg, who had already let herself in.

Startled, Julie tried to steady her breathing, but Meg took her arm and led her to a chair.

"Didn't your mother ever teach you to wait until the door is opened before you barge into someone else's house?" Julie was struggling to maintain self-control.

"The only thing I ever learned from my mother was that birth control was a novel idea," Meg cracked. But seeing Julie's pale face, she became serious. "You look like you've seen a ghost. What's going on, Julie? Are you okay?"

"I'm just a little shaken up, I suppose. Weird stuff is going on. I'm glad you could come." Julie detected a note of weariness creeping into her voice.

Meg ordered Julie to sit while she rummaged through the kitchen. "I'll make us something. Sorry to scare you. I figured you were expecting me. Kitchen door was unlocked. No, sit. You too, Fred. Su Li got you some chicken salad from the deli. I'll stuff that into a pita pocket with some alfalfa sprouts and tomato and you'll feel better in no time. Beats anything you'd make, anyway." Meg poured each of them a glass of Jumilla and continued. "Now, why are you so pale, and don't give me none of that I'm-a-redhead-skin-so-white-don't-tan business. Something had you spooked and it wasn't me coming through the kitchen door. Talk, girl."

Julie told Meg about the man who followed her, the call on the answering machine, the subsequent calls, and how Fred had growled just as Julie finished checking doors and windows, but at least that had been Meg. She was glad for her friend's presence. Meg was always sane and calm. This would never have rattled her, but her temperament and background were distinctly different from Julie's.

"So what are you supposed to confess to?" Meg asked.

"Who knows? When I first heard him on the answering machine, I thought it was pretty funny, you know, people dialing numbers randomly as a prank, so I confessed to having lustful thoughts about the new oboe player in rehearsal yesterday. You should see him, Meg, he's a doll."

"Getting over Jack already?" Meg queried wryly. She gave Julie an odd look.

"Hardly. He was just cute, that's all. Jack was my one and only. But what was really upsetting was that he called back two more times and *he knew my name*."

"Do you think it was the same guy that followed you?"

"That's a frightening thought. I hope not. That means he not only knows my name and phone number, he has an idea of right about where I live. What if he knows I'm alone as well? Want to stay with me until Su Li gets back? There's plenty of room."

"No thanks. No point in both of us being murdered in our sleep."

"Thank you. I knew I could count on you for comfort and support," Julie quipped. "Do you think I should call the police?"

Meg thought a moment, pressing her lips together and squinting. "Well, Julie, he hasn't done anything and you don't even know if it's the same guy. I mean, you could if you want to, but I doubt they'll do anything. What are you gonna say? Some nut case has been calling me and telling me to confess? They'd never take that seriously. Why don't you wait a while and see if anything happens? It's probably just some pervert who gets his jollies from upsetting women with stupid calls, and as long as he knows he's gotten to you, he'll keep it up." She laughed and continued, "Like this weirdo that called me a few weeks back, starts breathing real heavy, like he's having an asthma attack, and says, 'Hey baby, do you want what I'm holding in my hand?' And I just told him, 'Honey if you can hold it in one hand, then I don't want it.' He hung up on me so fast you'd've thought I was the one who made the call!"

Julie pressed her lips together and tried not to laugh at Meg's crude humor. She was starting to feel silly for overreacting. Meg was probably right. Julie wished she had more of the earthy life-is-not-so-serious-after-all attitude that characterized her friend.

A few minutes with Meg and she was feeling better. They filled their wine glasses again and tossed the bottle in the trash.

"On the other hand, Julie, what is it you think he might want?"

"Beats me."

"Don't suggest that to him," Meg giggled. "Let's play devil's advocate and assume for the moment that this is serious. What do you think he's after?"

Julie shrugged. "I would say valuables of some sort. I have jewelry, art, a few antiques and my instruments. But he sounded as if there was something more definite. Something specific. I can't imagine. He was so menacing. It makes me shiver just remembering his voice."

"It does sound as if there is something in particular. Think, Julie. Could it be something that was Jack's? What did you do with Jack's things?"

Julie was quiet, stunned to think this man could want anything of Jack's. "I gave his clothing to the church, except for a few sweaters and his favorite bathrobe, you know, stuff I couldn't bear to part with. I wear those things myself sometimes when the loneliness gets overbearing. They still smell faintly of his cologne. It makes me feel close to him again. His tools are in the garage by the Jaguar. Some of his books I gave to the library, but most I kept." Her voice trailed off. She had already dealt with this part of widowhood. She did not want these wounds re-opened. It was difficult to relive it with Meg.

"Did you go through his pockets before you gave his clothes away? What about the books? Did you leaf through the pages?"

"Meg! What a strange thing to ask!"

"It's just that maybe there was something of Jack's that was in a pocket or in a book. What about all his business records? Who has those, Julie?"

"Bill Simon took over Davenport Enterprises. He was Jack's right-hand man and always ran things when Jack was out of town, so I assume he has all those records. The business was set up so that in the event of Jack's death, I would get a monthly stipend and I do, so I've never thought that much about it. Jack seldom talked about his work with me. I still don't really understand what all Davenport Enterprises even does. He never kept any business records here at the house that I know of. He refused to bring the office home. He always said home was where your heart was and home was where he would find me."

"Touching."

Julie ignored Meg's sarcasm. "As far as his pockets and the books, I did go through them, but there was nothing that would even remotely mean anything to anyone."

"What was there?"

"There were a couple of photographs of me, and of us together, a symphony schedule, an itinerary from our last European tour as well as our upcoming tours, ink pens, business cards, just the usual stuff. Trust me Meg, nothing that would warrant being followed and harassed on the phone. Nothing out of the ordinary."

"Maybe he's a secret admirer. Maybe he's the new oboe player. Maybe somebody from your past. How many boyfriends did you have before you met Jack, anyway?"

"None. Jack was my one and only."

"You gotta be kidding. You're too pretty. You mean nobody, not even in high school?"

Julie started laughing. "My parents hosted a mixer at our house one night in an awful and ill-fated attempt to get me a date for an upcoming social event which I had no interest in attending. It was a disaster of epic proportions. Todd Sinclair. What a nightmare."

"What happened? I want details, girl."

"You may rethink that," Julie answered, taking a sip of her wine and relaxing as the deep red Spanish liquid warmed her. "First of all, Todd thought he was God's gift to women. I would have preferred a pony. Actually, if we're talking Todd, here, I would have preferred a root canal. Anyway, I am certain some unnamed culprit, likely my father, paid Todd to try to win my affection, so I would have a date for their la-de-da affair the next week. So he comes up to me and asks me to dance. I would have rather eaten a rat with bubonic plague, but my parents were present, so I politely accepted. In spite of dance lessons, I was not exactly the picture of grace as a teenager. The whole time we were dancing, he was asking me for a date. Yuk. I kept stepping on his shoes and we ended up tripping over each other's feet and fell into the swimming pool.

"He actually believed I did it on purpose and told me he thought it was sexy. What a jerk! Can you believe it? Then, he tried to French kiss me, double yuk, so I responded by trying to drown him. I felt it was justified. My father made me stop, which is too bad because I was winning. Anyway, the rest of the kids jumped in the pool to join in the fun, and things just continued in a downward spiral. Todd threw up in the pool, probably because I kicked him in the stomach after he made another pass, and of course, all that puke floating around caused quite a panic. It was hilarious, and for some reason, I never got asked out again. But in the end I won, because my parents grounded me for two weeks, which got me out of their dumb social event, so I stayed in my room and practiced my cello and giggled with Su Li."

Meg was howling. "So what became of Todd after that?"

"Beats me. His parents put him in another school. I never saw him after that, not that it broke my heart. So that's my big story of high school romance. I've had exactly two other semi-dates, which ended badly as well. I just wasn't cut out for romantic relationships. Until Jack, that is."

"So do you think you will date again?" Meg asked, chugging down her second glass of Jumilla.

"Never. Nobody could ever measure up to Jack. I have no desire to even try."

They ate their sandwiches and talked of other things. Meg offered her opinion that the caller would quit when he knew he could no longer upset Julie, and advised her to forget it.

"If it will make you feel better, I'll go through the house and check the doors, windows and all the rooms so you will know you're safe tonight. Okay?"

"I already checked the doors and windows, remember? That's what I had just finished doing before you scared me out of my skin."

"And yet, I came in the unlocked kitchen door and you never noticed. Did you look through the closets and under the beds? Behind the curtains? What about the basement?" Meg was thorough, if nothing else.

"Are you trying to frighten me?"

"No. I just don't want you to wake up at two in the morning and worry that you forgot to check something and end up calling me and disturbing my beauty rest." Meg grinned, causing her freckles to blend together across her cheeks and upturned nose. Her light brown hair was cut in a page boy and swung loosely above her shoulders. Her green eyes had taut stress lines at the corners from two disastrous marriages and a nightmarish childhood. Julie thought Meg would have been much prettier, that her features would have been softer, had her life been a little easier. She spoke with a slight country twang, and had a hardness about her that went beyond her athletic build and sharp personality. But Julie understood that Meg had been shaped by a difficult life, and she was happy to offer her sincere and caring friendship. She thought they balanced each other well.

"Okay," Julie agreed. "After all, you do need your beauty sleep. Far be it from me to encroach on something you've been missing out on for such a long time. Go on and check for monsters."

Meg threw a wet paper towel at Julie and said, "Just for that, you get to clean up the mess in the kitchen. Oh, I forgot, the princess never learned how to clean. You just take your paper towel and wipe down the counter and the table, back and forth like this." Meg swiped her hand over the counter in exaggerated demonstration. "Try not to strain your bowing arm. If you have trouble doing the dishes, just holler. I'll start upstairs and work my way down to the basement. Be back when I'm done."

"Thanks, Meg."

Half an hour later, the ever thorough Meg declared the house safe. "Want to crack open another bottle of wine?" she asked.

Julie had a two drink limit which she never exceeded. "It'll be getting dark soon, Meg. Two glasses is enough."

"Maybe for you, lightweight. I was just getting started."

"Sorry, girlfriend. No dice. Sure you don't want to spend the night?"

"No thanks," she replied, and left for home after instructing Julie to lock the door behind her and call her if the creep called back.

Julie went into the music room to practice. This room had been her favorite surprise in the house her husband built for her. Octagonal in shape, it had floor to ceiling windows around it with a view into the woods. The domed ceiling, with its hand-carved wood beams, added a rustic elegance. The room was acoustically ideal. The setting sun cast a soft orange and crimson glow through the west windows, blanketing the room in tranquil warmth. Julie loved practicing in her music room. On one side was her mother's ebony grand piano, and to its left, her cello, stand, and music cabinet. The room was sparsely furnished as Julie was the only one who used it. Su Li was allowed to come in to listen to her practice, but the music room was not open to others. This was Julie's sanctuary and the world at large, including Jack, was not welcome here.

Since there had already been symphony rehearsal this morning, Julie had not planned to practice her usual four to five hours. She began with slow scales, but found she was distracted and unable to concentrate. She questioned the wisdom of having two glasses of Jumilla. Her effort was half-hearted and finally, frustrated and disgusted with herself, she loosened her bow and put the cello back in its case. She was tired and fidgety, and feeling at loose ends when the telephone rang. She stiffened and felt her heartbeat quicken. She determined to not allow fear to be detected in her voice. Steeling herself, she gingerly picked up the receiver on the third ring and answered with a calm voice.

"Hey, Julie." It was Su Li. Her voice had always had a light song-like quality, but tonight it sounded heavy and lifeless.

"Su Li, I already miss you. How's Miyso?"

"Oh, Julie, she's so sick. I cannot bear it. You wouldn't recognize her. She's in so much pain, but still, she's fighting. I wish Wanh had told me sooner. The doctors say there is no hope, it's just a matter of time." Her voice cracked as Su Li fought for control.

"Su Li, I'm so sorry. I'm so very sorry. At least you can be with her now. I love your mother. She was always good to me and my family. I wish more than anything she was well. Is there anything I can do? Do you need anything?"

"No." Su Li sighed and regained her composure. "How are things at home? Everything okay?"

If only you knew. "Everything is fine, Su Li. Please don't worry about me. Concentrate on your mom. I miss you, but I managed not to blow up the kitchen or trash the house, yet. You just take care of Miyso."

"I will probably be gone for a month, maybe two, who knows?"

"Just keep in touch and let me know if you need anything. Tell your mom I love her. Now you go and get some rest. You sound tired."

"I am, Julie."

They hung up and Julie slowly climbed the winding staircase to her bedroom, her heart heavy and burdened. The master bedroom of The Monstrosity was large, light and airy. The walls, ceiling, carpet and window sheers were white. A king-size black wrought iron poster bed covered with a white comforter, pillows and sheets, invited romance and sweet dreams underneath a white gauzy canopy. The furniture was ebony. French doors led out onto a wide, curved cedar balcony displaying a spectacular view. Julie changed into her nightgown, finished getting ready for bed, and stepped outside onto the balcony into the cool night air.

She stood by the railing, breathing deeply, her eyes closed, willing the peace that pervaded the atmosphere to fill her. She opened her eyes to savor the beauty of this early summer night before it surrendered to darkness. The sun had just set, the last of its orange blush fading in the west. The only sound was the song of the crickets and the slight rustling of leaves in the gentle breeze as the nocturnal creatures stirred to life. Julie sat on the gliding swing and relaxed as peace settled her troubled spirit.

Night was falling quickly, but Julie sat quietly, unwilling to move. Her thoughts wandered back to the night she met Jack, their whirlwind romance and rush to marriage. Her friends told her she was crazy. They were right. She was crazy…crazy in love. They said it wouldn't last. They were right again, but for the wrong reason.

There had been a private, late afternoon performance for a few select corporations that were major supporters of the symphony. A meet and greet reception followed, which Julie reluctantly attended. The symphony members were strongly encouraged to attend these functions so they could meet some of the generous benefactors who ultimately paid their salaries and made their trips possible. She hated these receptions and believed the reward of being touched by beautiful music should be sufficient; however, skipping the social hour without good cause was frowned upon, so she attended, hoping no one would notice her and she could slip out early and go home. The symphony needed the corporate support, so she generally made an appearance, taking one for the team, as it were. She was alone and feeling awkward, impatiently waiting for the minimum time to pass when she could politely make her unobtrusive exit.

She discreetly glanced at her watch. If time flew when you were having fun, it really stood still if you were enduring torture. She put the watch to her ear to be sure it was ticking, but resisted the urge to hit it on her seat to see if doing so would make it beat faster. She was sitting by herself on a red velvet covered settee when a hand reached around from behind her offering a cup of punch. She turned and looked into the bluest eyes she had ever seen, smiling down at her from a tanned, handsome face.

"I thought you might like something to drink after such a stellar performance." He paused while she said nothing. "Not thirsty?" His smooth voice lilted with a faintly British accent, and his eyes sparkled, amused at the effect he was unmistakably having on her.

She squirmed and looked away. *Definitely European. Definitely older and far more worldly.*

Recovering quickly, Julie felt flattered by the attention, but this impending situation was not going to work. None of her futile attempts at relationships with men had ever worked and this man, suave, handsome, and oh-so-confident, was way out of her league. She felt like the high school bookworm that the captain of the football team deemed worthy of a greeting, only to ridicule her in front of the rest of the team. But she could not possibly be rude. For all she knew, this stranger was paying her salary.

"Yes, thank you. It's a bit dry on stage." She didn't recognize the voice coming from her mouth. It sounded like a little girl, a weak one at that. *Please just go away.*

The man handed her the punch, motioned to the vacant spot next to her on the settee and asked, "May I?"

Oh, if you must. She moved slightly to make room for him. She needed to quench any interest he was showing in her, but found at the moment, that she was having trouble breathing. This can never work, she kept repeating to herself, but the man was clearly not reading her mind.

"I can't decide whether the Rachmaninoff or the Tchaikovsky was my favorite," he chatted, totally oblivious to Julie's discomfort. "They both wrote with such romantic fever and emotion. Such passion! I suppose I could ask if you come here often, but I already know the answer to that." He smiled, his eyes twinkling down at her, increasing her discomfort even more. "It seems that I don't come often enough."

Julie was trying to find her voice, her real voice, and at the same time willing the hot, red blush she knew was all over her face and throat to disappear. She wished she had worn her buttoned up blouse and not the V-neck. She was always awkward around men and this was no exception.

"Are you hungry, by any chance?" he asked.

No. Not food. Not food. Just go away. Can't you see how miserable you are making me? Besides, I'm starved. Totally famished and my blood sugar is dropping like a rock. I never eat before a performance. But the words would not make the trip from her mind to her mouth, so she sat in uncomfortable silence.

A few of the other orchestra members passed by her, some trying to conceal their amusement at Julie's predicament, others envious of the attention that shy Julie was receiving from this urbane gentleman.

"I'm sorry. I've been rude. I'm Jack Davenport. I know your name is Julie Creighton. It's in the program. You know, it's a tad stuffy in here. Care to go out for a bit of fresh air?"

"In *this* neighborhood! Are you out of your mind?" Apparently, Julie had found her voice. *Could this day get any worse?*

He laughed, his white teeth gleaming and said, "I thought you had a bit of spirit. I could tell watching you play. I would be honored if you would accompany me to a new restaurant downtown that I discovered. Premio's. The food is excellent and the service unsurpassed. I don't bite, Julie. Really." His voice was gentle and inviting.

I'll bet. "I'm not really very hungry, thank you anyway. I was just on my way home. It was nice to have met you, Mr. Davenport. I'm glad you enjoyed the performance." She rose to leave and exited The Hall in a hurry.

Safe within her car, her cello strapped in the back seat, Julie headed home to the condo she and Su Li shared in the Central West End. It was not far from Duff's, one of her favorite restaurants, and, being ravenously hungry, she stopped to pick up her dinner to go. She ordered salad, an appetizer of toasted ravioli, chili, vegetarian stir-fry, whole grain rolls, and gooey butter cake for dessert. She hoped that would be enough. Performing gave her a voracious appetite, exacerbated by her habit of never eating before a performance. Su Li was away on a weekend retreat, so Julie was on her own for meals. That always meant take-out.

As she was turning to leave, bags of food in both hands, she heard a familiar voice. "I'd hate to see what you can put away if you ever do get hungry, or were you buying dinner for a family of eight? How do you stay so thin, anyway?" Behind her stood Jack Davenport, visibly amused to have caught Julie in a lie and grinning at the prospect of watching her try to squirm out of it. "There are tables outside. Mind if I join you?"

Julie suppressed a laugh. He certainly was persistent. She figured it couldn't hurt anything to eat one meal with this man. She wasn't far from home, and knew that after a few minutes of her company, he would be desperate to forget he'd ever met her. She seemed to have that effect on men.

"Okay."

He ordered a sandwich and two lemonades and they spent the next four hours talking. Jack watched in amazement as Julie ate every bite of her dinner, pausing to offer him one piece of toasted ravioli and a bite of gooey butter cake.

"You already know what I do for a living. What do you do?"

"I own Davenport Enterprises. We're located in West County."

"What type of business is that?" Julie had never heard of them.

"Mostly import-export. Boring stuff. I'd much rather talk about you."

Herself was the one subject Julie was least comfortable talking about, but Jack's low-key manner had a way of putting her at ease. They talked into the early morning hours, Julie telling him all about life at the conservatory, auditions, and how she ended up back in St. Louis. He learned she lived with her cats and her friend, Su Li, and she had never had a serious boyfriend, a fact he found nearly impossible to believe. By the time the sun was nearly rising, Jack knew almost everything about Julie there was to know, and the last thing he seemed to be was desperate to get away from her.

"You are the most fascinating and enchanting woman I have ever met, Julie Creighton. Not to mention beautiful." He was holding her hands, looking into her eyes, piercing her soul. "Please do me the supreme honor of agreeing to have dinner with me tomorrow night. If you say no, I will be crushed and may never recover."

"Well, I suppose we can't have you chronically ill. However, it's already tomorrow. Do you mean tonight tomorrow, or tomorrow tomorrow?"

"Tonight. I'll pick you up at seven." He kissed her lightly on the forehead and walked her to her car. "Try not to be too hungry tonight, Julie. I'd hate to think of needing to take out a corporate loan just to feed you." He held her hands while Julie contemplated kicking him in the shins, but he leaned down and brushed her cheek with his lips, so she let the thought go.

She had been unable to sleep that morning, as her heart raced with excitement and fear. What did he see in her? Maybe all these years she had been selling herself short. If she didn't get some sleep, she was going to look awful that evening. She turned over again in bed, punching her pillow in an effort to sleep. He said she was fascinating and enchanting…beautiful…

They ate at an elegant restaurant and then went dancing. Julie began to realize what the expression "swept off your feet" meant. She was falling for Jack, entering a new and frightening world. She was nervous and unsure of herself around him, feeling inadequate. He was strong and confident, so perfect. Julie feared he would tire of her and she would lose him. The night passed too quickly and soon he was walking her to her door.

"Would you like to come in for a cup of coffee?" she asked him before she remembered that, first, she didn't know how to make coffee, and second, since neither she nor Su Li drank coffee, there wasn't any in the kitchen. *How could I be so stupid?*

"I'd love some," he replied and held the door open for her. *Great. Now what? Think, Julie, it would be the first time you've done that in twenty-four hours.*

She ventured into the kitchen and rummaged through the pantry. There was nothing to drink but hot chocolate, tea or cooking sherry. "That Su Li. You know, good help is so hard to find these days. We seem to be all out of coffee. Sorry."

Jack was standing in the living room with a patient smile on his face. Julie was a poor liar. "That's all right. I wasn't very thirsty." He crossed over to her and put his arms around her. She leaned into him and he lifted her head and kissed her. The room started to spin as he probed her mouth with his tongue. He held her tightly and she felt herself tremble. His hand moved over the back of her dress and in one deft move, he unzipped her dress.

Julie's first reaction was disbelief. She pushed him away from her with a force she didn't know she had and started to back away, frightened. Her eyes were wide, her face paling as she felt the blood draining from her head. How could this be happening? What had she expected? She had really blown it this time. Jack was experienced and used to having what he wanted. But she couldn't, had never… And now, she would lose him for sure, this dashing, perfect man. Nevertheless, Julie was not ready for this, had never before encountered this situation, and had not dealt with anything other than dates that had been disastrous from the start. She had never been this embarrassed in her life.

Jack looked at her strangely for a moment, and then stepped toward her. "Julie, darling, I'm so sorry. Please forgive me. I am sorry." His voice was gentle, sincere and soothing.

Julie felt her eyes brimming with tears. She swallowed hard.

"Come here, Julie. It's all right. Come on. I apologize. I didn't mean to upset you. It's okay. I'm sorry, sweetheart." He reached around her, quickly zipped her dress up and led her to the sofa and held her. "I would never hurt you. I didn't realize—never mind. Please tell me you forgive me. I don't want to lose you. Not ever, especially over this. You mean too much to me."

Julie rested her head on his shoulder and tried unsuccessfully to restrain her tears. Jack stroked her hair and let her cry. "I'm sorry, Jack. I..."

"No, Julie. I'm the one who's sorry. It won't happen again, I promise. Now then, agree to a Sunday afternoon picnic with me tomorrow and I'll know I'm forgiven."

"A picnic?" Her mind reeled as she traded one angst for another. This could mean she had to cook. Su Li would not be home until Sunday evening. *This* would undoubtedly be the end of the relationship.

"Good. I'm forgiven. I'll take care of all the food. Why don't you make us a nice dessert? I'm dying to sample your cooking."

You'll more likely die if you sample my cooking. Julie's lack of culinary skill was one of the few things she had failed to mention when telling Jack her life story. *Why is life so hard?* "Sure. Name your poison." *Bad, but literal choice of words.*

"I love a good cherry pie."

"No problem." She smiled confidently. *Maybe I'll die in my sleep.* "See you tomorrow, Jack." He held her and kissed her one last time before leaving.

Panic stricken, Julie began frantically searching for a cookbook. Upon finding one in the kitchen of all places, she located a recipe for cherry pie. After reading it through nine or ten times, she made a grocery list and went to a twenty-four hour supermarket to buy her supplies before she would attempt to sleep. Of all the weekends for Su Li to be gone!

Unfortunately, Julie was unaware that when the recipe called for four cups of cherries, it meant canned or frozen tart cherries, not fresh Bing cherries. It took an hour and a quarter just to remove the pits and stems, and by the time the pie was finished, it was an unmistakable catastrophe. Julie had less than an hour left before Jack would arrive, anticipating a home cooked cherry pie. She quickly drove to Tippin's, purchased a cherry pie and got home with ten minutes to spare. She removed the pie from the box, pushing the empty box to the bottom of the trash can, and covered the pie with aluminum foil.

Jack arrived on time and they drove to Babler State Park in his Jaguar. He spread out a blanket and from the picnic basket he removed china, crystal, silverware, linen napkins and tablecloth, chilled wine, cheese, fruit, pate and crackers, seafood salad and an assortment of tiny sandwiches.

Julie's idea of a picnic was cold fried chicken, potato salad, and coleslaw. She was enthralled with Jack's concept of romance.

After lunch settled, Jack suggested, "Let's have some of that pie you made. My mouth is already watering. I can't remember when I last tasted homemade cherry pie."

That's too bad. But guilt-stricken, Julie cheerfully volunteered, "I hope you like it. It's one of my specialties." *Might as well go for broke.*

"Just like your coffee, I suppose," Jack said after the first bite. "Tastes remarkably like Tippin's." He lifted the pan where, on the bottom, clearly marked Tippin's, his suspicions were confirmed.

"Julie, darling," he sighed, leaning back on his elbows, "We've spent countless hours talking about everything under the sun. By any remote chance, have you once told me the truth about anything?"

Before she could answer, he leaned over and kissed her, long and hard. "What are you afraid of, Julie?" he asked softly, brushing her hair back with his hand.

Only everything. Life with you. Life without you. Being in love. Making love. Trusting you with my heart. Having it broken. You name it, and I'm probably afraid of it. "I'm not afraid of anything."

He took his forefinger and ran it down the bridge of her nose, then down her cheek. "Julie. I love you, you know."

"Why?"

He continued, ignoring the question. "There have been many women in my life, as you have guessed, but none have captured my heart until you. My business takes me all over the world and from all appearances I lead a full life. But my life was empty until Friday afternoon when I saw you walk onto that stage. I was drawn to you immediately. I had to get to know you. I have been completely captivated ever since. I was greatly relieved to find out you were unmarried and unattached." He continued, speaking slowly, deliberately. "I want to be with you all the time. I want you to trust me. If you trust me, there will be no room for fear in your heart. Please, Julie. Trust me."

She put her head on his chest feeling his strong arms envelope her. Had they really only known each other two days?

The night was clear and starry with a silver moon. Julie could hear owls in the woods, harmonizing with the crickets, serenading her with their soulful duet. The air was cool and still, refreshing and comforting on her skin. Julie rose from the glider swing and walked over to the balcony railing. She stood there quietly listening to the late-night music with heavy sadness rising slowly in her heart. She missed Jack all over again. How could she have even looked twice at that new oboist? There could never be anyone else for her. Jack was her one and only, the love of her life.

Why couldn't she appreciate the short time they had together for the gift it was? Would she ever reach the point where her memories would fill her with joy instead of sorrow? She felt cheated by his death, as though her brief happiness was nothing but a tease. Julie had many unanswered questions; questions she felt had no answers.

Their marriage had been short, but happy, filled with love, laughter, incessant teasing, music, and expensive gifts which Jack loved to lavish on his bride.

Julie turned and retreated into the bedroom to find Fred asleep on her bed with Sebastienne curled up next to him and Johann sleeping on the pillow next to hers. This was the usual nighttime arrangement since Jack's death. Pet hair was simply another fact of life. She smiled at her little darlings and climbed into bed. She knew that once she fell asleep, Fred would be up patrolling the house. Although he would always be nothing more than a lovable pet to Julie, Fred was, in fact, a well-trained guard dog, capable of attacking anyone he perceived as a threat, and this, not companionship, was the reason Jack bought him for Julie.

Stroking the big shepherd, she thought back to when Jack first brought Fred home.

"What is *that*, Jack?"

"I believe they call that a dog, darling."

"Thank you. I never would have guessed. The question, more specifically, for your rudimentary mind, is what is that dog doing here?"

"I got him as a gift for you, sweetheart. Isn't he beautiful?"

"Jack, darling, we already have two cats, and you have given me more gifts than I can ever repay."

"Juliette, every day with you is a gift."

"Oh, puleeeeeze!" She giggled. "I need a shovel and while you're at it, I'll take my hip boots, too. You really are too much. But for the record, sweetheart, I don't want a dog."

"Darling, I travel. Ergo, I'm not home all the time. This dog is trained to protect all that is precious to me, and that includes most especially, you. Now, you may name him, but there will be no compromising here on this issue. I will feel much better knowing you are safe when I'm not here."

"Jack, love, we live in the middle of nowhere. Nobody could find us even if they wished to do us harm. I see no need for a dog. Oh, no! He's been here only five minutes and he's already shedding! Look at the hair!"

"Dearest, no place can be considered safe these days. We live in dangerous times. And yes, I'm sorry to admit that of all the breeds in the world, nothing sheds like a German Shepherd. It's a small price to pay for a quality dog. But in no time, I am certain you will love him."

"Ugh! What is he doing!"

"He appears to be kissing your feet, darling. Not that I blame him. He likes you already. I heard he had good taste."

"Jack Davenport, that's disgusting. Make him stop!"

Johann and Sebastienne had ventured into the room to see what the commotion was all about. Sebastienne, the orange-flecked, black female, timid and petite, took one look at the giant monster and fled up the stairs at record speed. Johann, her large, orange brother, stayed to view from a safe distance this intruder on his territory. The dog padded over to investigate the cat, but Johann stood his ground. In a split second, a puffed out Johann hissed, raised his paw and firmly swiped the dog across his nose, eliciting a loud yelp and hasty retreat from same.

"Your dog has traumatized my cat! Oh, poor baby. Come to Mama, Johann. Did that big ol' dog scare Mama's kitty?" She picked him up and cuddled him.

"Julie, I believe it was your cat that scratched the dog. Johann appears quite unscathed. The dog, I wish you would name him, has a scratch on his nose and his feelings, I believe, have been wounded." The dog lay with his chin on the floor, a pitiful look of rejection on his face, and Julie felt her resolve begin to slip.

Jack stopped his lighthearted banter and became serious. "Julie, I've never asked you to do anything you didn't want to do. I've never insisted on having my own way about anything. You know that. But the dog stays. I do insist. I fear for your safety when I'm gone. He's no danger to the cats. Quite the opposite from what I've seen, but he will be excellent protection for you. His lines are exceptional, his temperament superior, and he has undergone extensive training. Now, will you please choose a name for him?"

Jack should have known better given Julie's proclivity for atypical names. Sebastienne was spelled with a feminine ending, Julie had explained to him, "So she won't develop a gender identity complex. I mean, how would you feel if you were a pretty little girl and they spelled your name S-e-b-a-s-t-i-a-n? Somebody has to think of these things, you know."

"I will name him Frederic, after Frederic Chopin, one of my favorite composers, but we will call him Fred, for short."

Jack looked sorry that he asked. A magnificent and terribly expensive animal as this deserved a noble, more befitting name. But Julie had spoken.

"Has he been neutered, Jack?"

"Heavens, no!"

"If the dog stays, the dog gets neutered. I do insist. There are enough unwanted puppies in this world, and heaven knows how many are dumped out this way only to die horrible deaths. Every pet should be wanted. It's a crime the number of puppies and kittens put to sleep every year just because of ignorant owners who won't be responsible to spay and neuter. I'll make the appointment in the morning. There will be no compromising here on this issue."

Jack looked a touch green, Julie thought, but within a week, Fred's propensity for fatherhood had been eliminated.

Julie bent down and kissed the dog's big, black, leathery nose. She stroked his head gently, thankful for his protection and companionship. She was tired and confused over the recent events. Her body yearned for sleep, but her mind continued to race, and sleep eluded her. She missed Jack. She missed Su Li. While it had felt good to return to rehearsal, she also felt a twinge of guilt for moving on with her life. She thought about her discussion with Pastor Grady and wondered if she might return to church and learn more. It had been a very long time since she had been to church. Pastor Grady's words returned to her. *God does not owe us an explanation. He is God and we are not...*

Thoughts of Miyso troubled her and she said a prayer for her, Su Li, and Wanh. It had been some time since Julie had prayed and her words faltered, but God knew her heart. Losing someone you loved was unbearably difficult. As Julie prayed, her own pain deepened, so she prayed more.

Eventually, weariness overtook her and she nestled down under the covers to sleep. However, she had been so immersed in thought she never heard the telephone ringing and fell into a deep sleep, unaware of the blinking light on the answering machine.

7

"Julie Davenport is being watched closely per my orders?" The man was short and compact, well built, with a dark mustache, dark eyes, and dark hair. His very presence exuded darkness, like a cloud hanging over the room. He sat behind a large desk, stroking his mustache with one hand, a sign he was in thought. "You informed me that she was followed home from rehearsal, correct? A man in a green Buick, yes?"

"That is correct, sir," his top agent replied.

"Do you have an opinion as to who this man might be?"

"I do, sir. Manny Tupelo drives such a car. He has expressed much interest in this matter. More than usual. I have informed him that I am on top of this and am fully capable of handling Julie Davenport."

"You are suggesting, then, that there is a rebel within our cause? A rogue agent, perhaps?"

"Perhaps, sir. Maybe someone who is overzealous, anxious to prove himself."

"Acting on one's own accord is unacceptable in this organization."

"Yes, sir."

"I will handle this. In the meantime, I need more information regarding Ms. Davenport. Your reports are of little help. Your reputation is one of thoroughness and efficiency. I expect better results."

"Yes, sir."

"You are dismissed."

The man was perturbed. If the pursuer in the Buick was Manny Tupelo, he was overstepping his bounds and would have to be dealt with. But Julie Davenport was the real problem. His best agent was unable to ascertain that which he most needed. Was she the key or was she a loose end to be eliminated? He could not have her taken out until he knew for certain. She could be valuable, extremely valuable. Maybe that was why she was holding her cards so closely. There had to be a way to find out for sure. She was an enigma to him. For now, however, there was another matter to be handled. He sent for Manny Tupelo.

"Yes, sir, I drive a green Buick."

"Did you attempt to follow Julie Davenport home?"

Manny swallowed hard. He looked sideways, obviously unprepared for this line of questioning.

"Do not lie to me. Do not ever lie to me. I will ask you again. Did you follow Julie Davenport home?"

"Yes, sir."

"This will not happen again. I run this organization. I am in charge. You have your orders. The others have theirs. If you find you cannot fulfill your own obligations and you take matters into your own hands, you will suffer consequences. Is that understood?"

"Yes, sir."

"You are dismissed."

Manny Tupelo was a small fry. There were dozens of Manny Tupelos, small time thugs with small mentalities, hoping for a shortcut to a big payoff, but having neither brains, nor talent, nor patience to reach their goals. True, he would have to be watched, but he was of no real concern.

Julie Davenport concerned him. The more he thought about her, the darker his mood grew. Although it was possible that she was totally innocent of any knowledge of the item, he doubted it.

He firmly believed she was keeping it in hiding, perhaps waiting for the highest bidder, perhaps waiting to see how it would be of the greatest use to her. He would not play that game with her. It was his, and he would have it. Where was it?

He began to formulate a new plan. There had to be another way to get what he wanted. If the likes of Manny Tupelo interfered, they would soon understand that tampering with the captain was not a smart idea.

Manny Tupelo stood outside and shook his head, puzzled. He could have sworn he wasn't followed. How, then, had he been found out? The captain had ordered him to drop the matter. He snorted at the thought. No way. There was too much at stake. Too much money. Too much power. They probably knew about the phone calls, too. There was nothing to tapping a phone anymore. No such thing as privacy for anyone. Cryin' shame. Your phone calls weren't even private nowadays.

The Davenport woman was the key to this whole thing. He had to have been close. Otherwise, the captain would not have been so upset with him. The next time she left for Powell Hall, he would go back. If she was in the city, he would have all the time he needed to find what he was looking for. It couldn't be that hard to discover exactly where the woman lived. He needed more information about her. The next time, he would be better prepared. And, he would make sure he was not followed.

Manny Tupelo stopped at a 7-11 to buy a newspaper and check out the symphony schedule.

8

Julie woke the next morning, sunlight flooding her bedroom, warming her, and rousing her from a deep and satisfying sleep. She knew she had overslept, but didn't care. Today was an off day for the orchestra, and Julie planned to stay home, practice and goof-off. She dressed in white shorts and an orange tank top, left her feet bare and trotted downstairs. Su Li would have had hot herbal tea ready if she had been home. Julie was sure she could make her own tea this morning. She just had to read the directions.

As she passed through the hearth room into the kitchen, she noticed the light blinking on the answering machine. "Never even knew it rang," she mumbled to herself as she pushed the button. It was him. This time he was angry and vulgar. He threatened to force her to confess. He was hard to ignore, as Meg had instructed her. He sounded as if he might be losing control.

She let the message play out, rewound and erased it. This was not going to bother her. Meg was right. He was just a creep and she had things to do today. She made a cup of tea after two attempts and poured a bowl of Cocoa Puffs, breakfast of champions. Chocolate. It's not just for breakfast anymore, Julie thought, silently chanting her chocolate mantra.

Julie completed her morning routine of pet and personal care and went into the music room to practice. The symphony was starting a "Back to Bach" series which Julie found difficult. She did not enjoy playing Bach. The mathematical precision with which he wrote clashed with the expression Julie sought to achieve in performance and she always required extra work when practicing Bach. She began with slow scales and then set up her music to begin. Halfway through her practice, the doorbell chimed. Julie, who seldom heard her own doorbell, since the few people who came to visit rarely used it, would have ignored its ringing had it not been for Fred's incessant barking. Aggravated at having her practice time interrupted, Julie rose to answer it.

On the porch stood a man Julie's height with soft brown eyes, a full mustache, dark hair and a calm demeanor.

"Good morning, Mrs. Davenport?"

"Yes. Who are you?"

"I'm Detective Sam Hernandez with the Pineview Police Department. May I speak with you for a few moments?" He was polite and soft spoken.

"You don't look like a policeman," Julie replied, more flippantly than she intended.

Detective Hernandez started a bit and blinked, obviously not anticipating her remark, and suppressed a grin. Julie didn't exactly look like a symphony cellist either, dressed in shorts, a tank top, and barefoot. She eyed him uncertainly and looked beyond him to the driveway where his grey sedan was parked under the canopy behind him. He smiled slightly.

"We don't always wear uniforms or drive squad cars, Mrs. Davenport. Here is my card. You may certainly call the number to inquire about me. I would like to speak with you about your late husband's accident. May I come in?"

Julie felt the color drain from her face as her knees weakened. "Of course."

"Will you please put your dog up?" Fred continued to growl, displeased with the unknown visitor.

"I will have him sit, but he stays with me at all times." Julie remembered Jack's warnings to her and she was grateful for Fred's protection. "Please come in and sit down." She opened the door to allow the man in and gave the dog a command. Fred sat quietly on the sofa next to Julie, keeping a guarded eye on the guest. She wished Su Li was here to bring her something to drink. She felt too unsteady to go into the kitchen herself.

"Are you all right, Mrs. Davenport? You're not ill?"

"I'm fine. I—I haven't discussed Jack's accident since the first investigation six months ago. I have been trying to put it all behind me and go on. This is rather unexpected."

"Mrs. Davenport, I'm sorry to have to bring all this up again, but the investigation has been ongoing and there are some strange circumstances surrounding your husband's accident."

"What do you mean, strange? It was a routine business trip. Jack traveled frequently in his line of work. His engine failed and he crashed into a mountain. It was horrible, but how is it strange?" Julie felt as if the room was tilting. For months she had found the accident hard to accept. Jack was a careful pilot, meticulous in every detail, from the safety check on the plane, to filing the flight plan, to checking the weather.

"How frequently did your husband travel?"

"About every six to eight weeks. He always flew the jet himself. He was a skilled pilot."

"Where did he go? Do you know who he saw?"

"He frequently went to California, sometimes Canada, sometimes New York. He just saw business contacts, that's all. He was never gone more than a few days and he called me every night. I don't understand why you are asking me these questions."

"I know this is difficult, Mrs. Davenport," his voice was low and calm, his manner gentle, and Julie imagined he was a kind person with an unpleasant job to do. "Can you tell me about your husband's business? What did he do?"

"He owned and ran Davenport Enterprises. It was an import-export business in West St. Louis County."

"Where in West County is it located?"

Julie raised her eyebrows as she realized she had never been to Jack's office, a fact which had never before struck her as odd.

"Actually, I don't know, exactly. Jack never really talked about his work. He always said I would find it boring to listen to him talk about trading different types of goods, discussing the stock market, and all that. I assumed he was probably right. I don't have much interest in that sort of thing, so I would ask him how his day went and he would say fine, and that was about it. He preferred to leave work at work because there was more to life than a job. He often told me that.

"Whenever we would have lunch together, we always met at a restaurant. Between his schedule and my performance and practice schedules, we rarely saw each other during the day. He was always home promptly at 5:30 and didn't work weekends. To answer your question, I've never been to the office. But I know he was there. I called him on occasion. Why are you asking these questions? What does any of this have to do with his accident?"

The more Julie talked, the more alarmed she became, not only at the carefully formed questions this man was asking, but also at her own haltingly given answers, which were vague. She sounded as if she was trying to avoid the subject, while at the same time understanding how little she actually knew of Jack's business affairs.

"Did you ever accompany him on his business trips?"

"No. He never asked me to. He called me every night. I almost always had symphony performances when he traveled."

"So his business trips coincided with your performance schedule?"

Julie frowned at the connection she thought he was trying to make. "I guess I never gave that much thought, but yes, frequently they did."

"What goods did your husband import and export? Do you know what countries he was importing from or what countries he was exporting to?"

Julie was quiet for several moments. She looked down at her hands, twisting her wedding rings and answered softly, "I don't know. Jack seldom talked about work."

"Was Mr. Davenport's life insured?"

Julie looked up. Finally, a question she could answer. "Of course. Jack saw to it that I was well taken care of."

"Mrs. Davenport, how much insurance money did you receive?"

"Two million dollars. I also receive a monthly stipend from Davenport Enterprises," Julie replied quietly. She fingered her wedding rings again, realizing how her answers must have sounded to this stranger.

"Mrs. Davenport, did your husband have any enemies?" Detective Hernandez' soft voice never wavered. It was subdued throughout his questioning, but the weight of his words fell heavily on Julie.

God in heaven, someone murdered Jack and they think it was me! How can this be happening? Don't they know how much I loved him? What is going on here? Julie's mind was racing at the implications, incredulous that anyone could think her capable of hurting Jack. She felt her breathing quicken as blood rushed to her head, causing it to throb. She wished more than ever that she was not alone. "You're telling me my husband's plane crash was not an accident?" Her voice was shaky and her head was getting lighter.

"There is reason to believe it may not have been an accident. The investigation is still in progress. We are trying to make sense of some things that don't fit together right now. Was your marriage happy? You were married less than a year, is that right? Did you find it difficult making the adjustment to married life?"

He's good, really good. But his gentle manner could not belie the ugly insinuations she sensed beneath its surface. "We were very happy together, Detective Hernandez. We were very much in love. Jack was my life and I was his. We were supposed to grow old together and have children and grandchildren and memories, but now you're telling me it was not an accident that took those things away. It was a deliberate act of violence? Well, Detective, although I find it difficult to believe, my husband obviously did have at least one enemy, didn't he? I hope for his sake, you find him before I do."

Julie's answer started quietly, not much above a whisper, but as his insinuations sunk in, and the more she spoke, the more passionate she became and the vehement crescendo with which she finished her reply surprised even her. Trying to manage her grief had been an arduous ordeal when she believed Jack's death was an accident. Now she shook with anger at some unknown person or persons who intentionally took her beloved from her.

"Mrs. Davenport, I am sorry to have upset you. That was not my intent. Your husband was a wealthy and powerful businessman by all appearances. His plane accident is suspicious and we are unable to locate his place of business. In fact, there is no record of Davenport Enterprises in any of the St. Louis County municipalities or the state of Missouri. The Secretary of State's office has no listing for your late husband's company. Davenport Enterprises, along with all of its assets, liabilities and employees has either vanished or never existed in the first place. You are the only connection to Jack Davenport we can find. You claim you receive a monthly stipend from the company. How is this payment made?"

I didn't claim it, I get one! "I receive an automatic deposit into my savings account." Julie rose to get herself a glass of water, which was a mistake. The room began to spin, then everything went dark and Sam Hernandez, bolting from his chair, caught Julie before she struck her head on the coffee table.

She awoke a few minutes later to the sound of Fred growling and barking, and weakly ordered him to sit. She tried to sit up but felt as if her body was made of jelly and fell back against the sofa cushions. Detective Hernandez brought her a glass of water and offered assistance in sitting up, both of which Julie gratefully accepted.

He placed his card on the coffee table and said, "Mrs. Davenport, here is my phone number. Please call me any time if you remember anything at all regarding this matter. I will return at a later date, but I believe you have had enough of a shock to deal with at this time. There are still many unanswered questions. Again, I am sorry to put you through this." He saw himself out and Julie was left alone, her head still spinning.

Sam Hernandez stopped his car in the same copse of trees from which Julie had watched her pursuer two days previously, took out his note pad and began writing his impressions. Julie Davenport had provided him with few facts he had not already known and no helpful evidence or information. He believed she had not told him a number of things, but he had been greatly disconcerted by how white she became. He knew she suffered genuine shock. This also puzzled him. Wives usually knew something was going on, even if they were not directly involved themselves. Julie Davenport was not stupid, yet she seemed completely unaware of anything involving her husband's business. Frustrated, he now had as many questions as he had an hour ago. He unconsciously stroked his mustache as he jotted his initial impressions:

Julie Davenport – Involved and covering up? Totally inno-cent? How?
Upset/distraught at mention of:
Accident - normal or guilty?
Suspicious circumstances- normal or guilty?
Unable to locate Davenport Enterprises – vague
Good actress or genuine?
Admitted to 2 Mil in Life Ins.
If innocent, is she in danger?

His last question disturbed him more than the others. His interrogation of her did not go as he thought it would. He put the car in gear and left. He had their conversation on tape and would go over it again when he reached his office.

9

How can this be happening now? I don't need anything more to deal with. Haven't I been through enough? What is going on? Julie had a headache. She picked up Detective Hernandez' card and studied it. Navy blue print on white. Pineview Police Department, Detective Samuel Hernandez. There were two office numbers in addition to a voice mail number, cell phone number and a dispatch number, so she could never claim she couldn't reach him. Detective Hernandez was the most accessible man she had met.

Was it possible Jack's accident had been arranged? The more Julie thought about it, the more she became convinced this was so. Otherwise, the police would not still be continuing their investigation, would they? Jack was too careful, too safety conscious. But why would someone want to kill him?

Jack was philanthropic to a flaw. Generous, friendly, outgoing, he was always willing to give someone a hand or a second chance. This was crazy. But if it was true—if someone murdered Jack, then Julie needed answers.

Unfortunately, she knew almost nothing about Jack's business affairs. He never wanted to bore her with the details of import-export, and she had never pushed for any. Had Jack been hiding something from her? No way. No way would she doubt her husband, especially when he could not defend or explain himself. But there was the green Buick, the phone calls, and now, Detective Hernandez. She could not explain those, either.

"Okay, Julie, get a grip. Gotta start somewhere." She was talking to herself again. She did know where Jack had stored the jet. There was a small, little-used airstrip about a half-hour drive from home. Julie knew that Jack always used the same mechanic, a man he trusted to maintain his plane. His name was Rich, or Rick, something like that. She would ask around. It wasn't like she was going to Lambert International Airport. How many mechanics and employees could a tiny local airstrip have, anyway?

She let Fred out while she changed clothes and put her cello away. Just as she reached the door to leave, the phone rang. Her body stiffened. But then she relaxed. This was her house and she was in charge. Calm, cool, collected and with a good night's sleep behind her, this creep was going to get an earful. She snatched the receiver with resolute firmness, fully prepared to blast him. But it was Meg's voice on the other end.

"Hey, what's doin'?"

"Meg, I was just on my way out."

"Rehearsal? I thought you were off today."

"No, just some miscellaneous errands. With Su Li gone, I thought I'd see what the common folk do." Julie hoped her joking would placate Meg. She did not want to tell Meg about these latest developments. What was the point? She didn't know anything herself, and she was uncomfortable with the questions Meg put to her last night. She knew Meg was trying to be helpful, but Julie didn't feel like answering anything else until she had some answers herself.

"Well, Princess, common folk cook their own meals after they run errands, or am I overwhelming you?"

"No, I'm not overwhelmed, just whelmed, thank you very much."

"You're welcome. By the way, do you pump your own gas, or do you only do full service?"

"Funny. I've been pumping my own gas for years. I just had to read the instructions a few times, that's all."

"Thought so. So where are you off to?"

"Oh, here and there, no place special. What's up with you?" Julie was purposely vague and anxious to leave.

"I was just wondering if you heard any more from our friend the phone geek."

"One more time on the machine," Julie replied. "I was out like a light last night and never even heard the phone ring. I can deal with him."

"Ok. You go run your errands. Call me if you need me."

They rang off and Julie let Fred back in the house and headed out the door. This time, she would be extra cautious to watch for strange cars and people, but she saw no one.

After a few wrong turns, Julie finally reached McGarret's Airfield. It was more rundown than she remembered, but she saw a few planes that looked well cared for. She walked into the office, which smelled of stale smoke and was definitely dirtier than she remembered. A man in his mid-thirties greeted her... sort of.

"Yeah?"

"Hello. I'm looking for one of your mechanics. I think his name is Rick or Rich, something like that?"

"Ain't nobody here named Rick or Rich, or something like that," he grunted.

Great. Mr. Helpful. Just what I need. "He was the mechanic here that worked on my husband's Lear jet," Julie explained. "My husband's name was Jack Davenport. Please, this is important."

"Hold on. I'll look it up." He heaved himself out of the chair and walked to a file cabinet. Julie noted he needed a shave, a haircut, and clean clothes. His dirty jeans sagged in the back and his plaid shirt was unbuttoned, revealing a torn undershirt. This place had gone downhill since she and Jack were last here. The man returned with a log book and began flipping pages. "Your husband's jet was maintained by Russ Richards."

That was the name. Now she remembered. "May I speak with him, please?"

"Ain't possible."

Julie felt her blood pressure rise and her pulse quicken. This man was straining her ability to remain civil. "Why not?"

"He don't work here no more. Record book says he never came back from vacation. Had a problem with the bottle, ya know. Prob'ly went off on a binge, and when he came back was prob'ly shown the door. Cain't tolerate no drunks workin' on them planes. But he ain't been here in months. I don't know nuthin' else."

"What about an address or phone number?"

"Ain't got that information. Lady, er Ms. Davenport, the guy was a bum. Knew his aircraft real good, great mechanic and all that, but he drank too much. He's prob'ly moved six times by now. Sorry."

Terrific. Now what? "May I use your phone, please?" Julie had a car phone for emergencies, but had no interest in owning a cell phone. She did not believe anyone should be tied to a phone, nor did she feel it necessary to make herself available 24 hours a day. Pay phones were disappearing, but she was determined to remain cell phoneless.

"Knock yourself out." He shoved the phone to the edge of the desk where she could reach it.

She would talk to Bill Simon at Davenport Enterprises. Bill could straighten things out. She probably should have started with him anyway. But when she called the number, a recorded message informed her that it was not a working number. Detective Hernandez was right. Her husband's company had either vanished or never existed at all.

Julie needed chocolate. She hadn't had any since breakfast; it was past one in the afternoon and she had not eaten lunch. Although it was at least an hour's drive, Julie wanted quiche from Andre's. That sounded delicious. Quiche Lorraine, salad, iced tea and a chocolate rum ball for dessert. Andre's would be perfect, and well worth the long drive. She needed time to think.

She thanked the man for all of his help and left, driving toward the highway.

She arrived at her favorite lunch spot, taking in the quaint, but authentic Swiss accoutrements that Andre and his wife brought with them when they emigrated from Switzerland. The tea room was nearly empty, with less than an hour remaining before closing, but the rich familiar smells that filled the air assured Julie there was plenty of food remaining. She ordered quiche Lorraine, green beans and salad. European rolls and freshly brewed iced tea were included with each lunch. When the dessert tray was presented, she didn't think twice before choosing the chocolate rum ball, studded with chocolate shot all over. The perfect ending to her favorite meal.

Lunch was excellent and refreshing, as expected, and Julie purchased a box of her favorite pastries from the sumptuous bakery case to take home. She loved Andre's butterflies, the beautifully shaped puff pastry with a light sugar glaze, and the chocolate pistachio cakes. And of course, the rum balls. She drove home, meandering along the back roads, pondering all that had happened. She came up with nothing but dead ends and more questions. *Where do I go from here?*

Sam Hernandez sat in front of Joe Spence's desk and listened to the tape of his conversation with Julie Davenport for the third time.

"I'm not buying this, Sam," his supervisor told him. "She was his wife, for Pete's sake. This lady is a professional cellist with a world class symphony. Graduated third in her high school class and fourth in college. She's too smart to be this dumb."

"I'll keep trying, Joe, but my gut instinct tells me she really doesn't know anything."

"So you've said," Joe Spence replied drily, his brows knit together in a frown. Sam was one of his best men and he respected his opinion enough to not undermine it, at least not yet. "You're the one who was with her and saw her. I'll accept that for now, but keep poking. She knows something, I'd bet the rent. We know the package never reached its destination. We also know that a great deal of money was spent for its purchase. Don't forget, the lady has two million reasons for helping herself to widowhood."

"Definitely the wrong angle, Joe. She was very much in love with her husband. She's still working through her grief, even though she claims she's past that point. I saw genuine shock register all over her face and the faint was real. Fake faints are easier than anything to spot. Have you considered that if she is innocent, she could be in grave danger? I think we should put someone on her a little more closely."

"We'll know if she's in trouble," Joe said, dismissing Sam's concern. "If she knows anything, or if she has the package, it'll spook her if she thinks she's being watched. In the meantime, just keep pushing. I put her financial information, her social calendar and whatever background information I got so far in a folder on your desk. Keep digging. Study that folder. Something will click. In the meantime, Keisha will transcribe the tape recordings."

As he poured over the paperwork, the more Sam Hernandez learned about Julie Davenport, the more he believed Jack Davenport had found the perfect woman to be his wife. But how she fit into his schemes, he did not know. Jack Davenport was dead and Julie had spent her entire life with her nose in music books, far removed from the cares of the real world. She had grown up with money and privilege, never needing to bother with the details of everyday living. When a dashing, exciting, older man came into her life and didn't want to "bore her" with the details of his business, she was content with whatever else he had to offer her. Probably romance, expensive gifts, a sufficient social calendar, a feigned interest in her music, and whatever else he believed would make her happy and keep her wherever it was he needed her.

Sam had to know more.

How did a dangerous man like Jack Davenport meet a classy lady like Julie, and why did he marry her unless she could be of some use to him? And how was it she never caught on to his game? Or did she?

Deep in thought, he stroked his mustache. He knew his answers would come in time. Either she would make a move, or, worse yet, what he was beginning to fear, someone would make a move against her. He needed to be patient. No problem. If he was anything, Sam Hernandez was a patient man.

Julie drove toward home and up the winding path to her garage without being followed. She was careful to be observant. Her search for answers had proven unproductive. Time to go home and regroup. She pulled her Maxima into the garage and parked next to the Jaguar. When she got out of her car, she looked in horror at the interior of Jack's car. Someone had been in the garage. Someone had taken a knife or some other sharp object and completely destroyed the seats, removed the glove compartment and stereo, and ripped the entire interior to shreds.

Fearful that the intruder may be in the house, Julie backed out of the garage and started down the hill. Had her pets been harmed? She could not bear the thought. Shaking, she called 911 from her car phone and waited nervously until a squad car pulled in behind her.

A uniformed officer got out and Julie showed him the Jaguar, explaining she found it like that when she arrived home.

"Have you gone inside your home, Ma'am?" he asked her.

"No. I was too frightened. I still am. I thought that whoever did this may still be in the house."

"Okay, that was smart. I'll call for back up and we'll go in together to check."

Within minutes, two more squad cars pulled up, ready to take on the only action in sleepy Pineview that week. After the police examined the Jaguar and took some notes, they accompanied Julie into her home. At first glance, everything seemed normal, but soon, Julie noticed little things out of place.

"There's some flour on the countertop," she told the officer. *Where is Fred?*

"You're sure you didn't miss it when you last baked?"

"Trust me," she remarked drily. "I don't cook very often." She began to pull drawers out. "The things in these drawers have been moved around. Someone was here, but tried to make it so I wouldn't notice." The officer took notes as Julie spoke, but did not comment. "Where's Fred?"

"Who's Fred?"

"My dog!" She called his name several times, running through the house, and found him lying in an upstairs bedroom, groggy. "Fred! How could you sleep through this? You're supposed to be a guard dog!" she scolded. Fred struggled to stand and collapsed.

"Ms. Davenport, your dog's been drugged," the policeman said to her.

"*What?*"

"Your dog. He's been drugged. Look at him," the officer replied. It was true. Fred's eyes were bleary and despite his attempts to stand, he faltered. As Julie rushed to him, he lay down and went back to sleep. "I think he'll be okay, ma'am. He probably just needs to sleep it off. If he was given a fatal dose of whatever it was, it would be too late by now."

"How did they get in? This house was locked tighter than a drum."

"There's no sign of forced entry, ma'am. Who else has a key to your house?"

"Only my friend, Su Li Tuan. She lives here with me. She would never give it to anyone. But she's out of town now, anyway. I have the only other key. I checked all the doors and windows just last night. Everything was locked."

One of the other officers entered the room. "All doors and windows were locked except one in the dining room. That had to be the point of entry."

"Impossible." Julie felt as if she would lose control any minute. Her head began to throb.

The policemen looked at each other without emotion and one said, "It's locked now, Ms. Davenport. Can you tell us if anything is missing?" Julie quickly went through the house. Her jewelry and all her other valuables seemed to be in place, but she was acutely aware that someone had been in all of the rooms in her home. It was obvious they were looking for something Julie did not consider valuable. Even her wall safe had been found, but her chocolates had been untouched. *Proves it was a man.*

"Ma'am, we've been through the whole house. Whoever was here is gone now. We'll file a report and let you know if there are any developments. Meantime, call us if you need us."

Yeah, right. "Thank you for coming."

The officers left and Julie went back upstairs to check on Fred. She stroked his big head, and his tail wagged sluggishly. Several minutes later, he was up, shaking his head, trying to shake off the effects of whatever had been given to him.

Julie went to her bedroom to lie down and predictably, found the cats hiding under the bed. Someone had been in this room. What were they looking for? She felt violated, and thinking about Jack's car made her sick to her stomach. What a waste. She wished Su Li were here. Her headache was getting worse.

Exhausted, Julie drifted off to restless sleep, but was awakened by the doorbell. Groggily, she got up to find Sam Hernandez at her door...again.

"Mrs. Davenport, are you all right?" She thought he sounded concerned. "I hear you had an intruder this afternoon. I came by to see how you were doing."

He seems so much more human than the officers that were here earlier. "Um, yes, um...I'm sorry, I fell asleep...too much stress, I guess. I'm fine. A little shaken up, I suppose. Nothing seems to have been taken, but the house was gone through and my husband's car was trashed. Fred was drugged, but he seems okay, now." Fred was by Julie's side, staring at the detective, as though he had caught him stealing a treat.

"I can see that."

"He makes you nervous? Sit, Fred." Julie smiled. Detective Hernandez seemed so nice.

"Anybody that looks at me as if I was his favorite meal makes me nervous." He smiled back at her. "May I come in, Ms. Davenport?"

"Sure. And you can call me Julie."

"Thanks, Julie. I'm Sam, if that will make you more comfortable. And, for the record, I will be taking on this case. I don't want to upset you any more than you already are, but this break-in may be related to your husband's plane crash."

Julie smiled weakly. "I'm already on emotional overload, so you might as well tell me that this also ties in with whoever shot President Kennedy and kidnapped the Lindbergh baby. I guess I'm ready to believe about anything by now."

"Do you feel up to talking, Julie? I promise to leave the minute I overstay my welcome."

"Sure." Julie brought in a pitcher of iced tea and the pastries she had brought home from Andre's. It never hurt to build up your energy.

"Tell me how you and your husband met."

His manner was friendly, gentle and easy going. Julie found it impossible not to talk with him. It had been a long time since she had really talked about Jack. She was afraid it would be too painful. Some of it was, but as the memories came flooding back, she realized how good it felt to share them with someone who seemed genuinely interested.

Sam listened attentively, absently stroking his mustache, thinking over all Julie was telling him. She talked about Jack, the house, her pets, Su Li, the symphony and music in general. The more she talked, the more he realized how lonely she was. Lonely and vulnerable. Make that lonely, vulnerable and beautiful. He would hate for something to happen to her.

He looked at his watch. "Julie, may I bother you for some more lemon for my tea? Thanks."

When Julie went into the kitchen, Sam Hernandez quietly slipped a new tape into his recorder and deftly planted a bugging device under the mahogany and marble coffee table. When she returned, he was sitting exactly where he had been when she left him. He smiled at her.

"Julie, what personal effects did Jack leave behind?"

"Nothing too exciting. Jack was fastidious. Before I gave away some of his things, I went through the pockets. In case there was something important, you know, but there wasn't. Just the typical stuff."

"What kind of typical stuff?"

"Photos of me, photos of us together, business cards and pens, a symphony schedule, an itinerary from the last European tour the symphony played. That's about it. Nothing to write home about. Certainly, nothing to warrant a break-in."

"Did you keep any of those things?"

"Actually, yes. When I went through Jack's things before taking them to the church, it was so hard to part with anything, I ended up keeping some stuff, mostly because throwing it away seemed too final. Do you really want to see all that?"

He nodded. "If you don't mind and it's not too much trouble."

She left him alone in the living room. He looked around and planted more bugs. Her home was immense. Everything in it exuded expensive taste and plenty of money to satisfy it. Thick, Palladian carpeting, soft, muted colors of beige, sage green, and peach dominated the decor. He had never personally known anyone who actually lived like this. In spite of Julie's "lean years," she had never known want. However, he reflected, she seemed unspoiled by wealth. Or maybe this was what was meant by being to the manor born. Her material possessions must not mean too much to her, he mused, since she allows that dog full run of the house.

Julie returned with the items Sam asked to see. The business cards were for a printing company, a floral shop, a Belgian chocolatier and a musical instrument repair shop. The symphony schedule could have been picked up anywhere, but he noticed that the itinerary from their European tour was marked in faint, barely perceptible pencil with small ticks.

"Are you familiar with these businesses?" he asked, showing her the cards.

"Yes. The printer, I assume, is who he used for Davenport Enterprises, although I'm not sure of that. The florist has been our favorite since we began dating. Jack regularly had fresh flowers delivered here. The chocolates are a special standing order that I receive every Valentine's Day, and as far as the music shop, Arturo has worked on my cellos since I was a child. He's practically a grandfather to me."

"I see. Do you mind if I take these things? I promise to return them."

"Keep them. I meant to throw them out. It was just hard to part with anything of Jack's, but I have no need of them." She paused a moment, then continued, "On second thought, I would like the photos returned."

"Of course. Thanks. Did your husband accompany you on your European tour?"

"Oh, yes. I was so glad he could come! Our tours can be exhausting and Jack made everything fun and romantic. You know, he knew his way all over Europe. After all, he grew up in England. Or was it Wales or Ireland? You know, I don't think he ever said. Just Europe," she shrugged. "It was wonderful he could be flexible enough to travel with me. He would personally oversee my instrument, which made things a lot easier on me."

"How were the symphony instruments usually handled?"

"Some instruments, of course, are small enough to be hand carried. My cello, though, and the other large instruments, would be listed, and they go in their cases inside another large specially made case which is shipped and travels separately. They show up back stage at the concert hall. Then we take them out and play them, and put them back in. The cases might come to the hotel room on occasion, though. You don't get a lot of practicing time on tour, which is why I appreciated Jack's thoughtfulness on our last tour. I had my cello with me most of the time."

"Don't your instruments go through customs?"

"Oh, sure. Sometimes, the customs agents look through the cases, sometimes they don't. There have been a couple of orchestra members who have put jewelry, caviar, wine, that kind of thing, in their cases. When those people get caught, it's bad news for everybody. Most of the time, however, nothing is in those cases except what's supposed to be."

"Has your case ever been opened?"

"Yeah. At one point or another, practically all of us will get picked for inspection. On this last tour, for that matter, my case was chosen. They found my cello, two bows, resin, a soft cloth and two extra sets of strings. Real exciting stuff."

Sam smiled. "What about the break-in this afternoon? What can you tell me about that?"

"Didn't you read the police report? Everything should be in that," Julie replied. She looked to Sam as if she was beginning to tire.

"I'd like to hear it one more time from you. Sometimes people remember things they didn't consider to be significant. You've had a little time to reflect, and you may remember what happened a little differently if you tell it again."

Julie left out the part about going to McGarret's Airfield and the number at Jack's company being out of service. She assumed Sam knew about the phone number anyway. Those endeavors turned out to be dead ends, so she told him she had run errands and treated herself to lunch at her favorite tea room. She offered him pastries, evidencing same.

"And you still have no idea what this person was looking for?"

"Clueless."

"Julie, is there anything you can remember that you haven't told me yet?"

Plenty. Are you aware that there are a lot of nut cases out there? Is there anything you haven't told me? "Nothing comes to mind," she answered with the innocence of a child just discovering a daisy.

"Please call me if you remember anything else, or if I can be of assistance to you in any way. You still have my card?" He left another on the coffee table just in case.

"Yes. Thank you."

Sam walked to the door, nodded goodbye, and left. Although he was now more certain than ever that Julie did not have the information he sought, he was also certain she had not told him all she could have. He wanted to trust her. He also wanted her to trust him. What was she holding back, and why?

Sam knew how to get suspects to open up and talk without them ever realizing that his friendly, unassuming conversation was an effective method of eliciting the very information they sought to keep to themselves. He felt as though Julie were playing a cat and mouse game with him. Yet, at the same time, he was seeing her less as a suspect—so what was the secret she was keeping from him?

Eventually, he would find out. He had the tapes of their conversation and the bugs he planted would pick up anything said in the main floor of the house, at any rate.

Julie was spent. Too much had happened in one day. She had planned on spending several hours working on the "Back to Bach" series, and now it was too late. She checked the answering machine, but neither Meg nor Su Li had called. Neither had her secret admirer. No news was good news. She sank into Jack's easy chair with her box of Belgian chocolates. At this rate, she would be out of them well before next Valentine's Day. She picked out a milk chocolate covered chocolate butter filling, laced with a touch of Amaretto. She put it into her mouth, closed her eyes, and slowly sank deeply into the chair. The creamy chocolate outside and soft chocolate filling kissed with Amaretto blended harmoniously together in a symphony of pleasure, coating her tongue with its satiny aphrodisiac, floating on clouds of cocoa. The faint hint of almond teased her senses and calmed her as she surrendered to its rich, silken chocolate paradise...

He was stroking her hair, softly, gently lifting it up and letting it fall back into place. His hands moved to the back of her neck and tenderly began massaging it, releasing all of her tension.

"You've had a hard day, Juliette," he whispered.

Silently, he massaged her temples and ran his finger down her nose. He caressed her cheek with the back of his fingers and kissed her closed eyelids. He lightly kissed the bridge of her nose, then her cheeks, her chin, her neck. His tongue moved in little circles all over her neck, sending a chill down her spine.

"I need you, Jack. I need you here with me now."

She put her arms around his neck and he held her tightly, his breath hot and rapid over her ear, his hand moving slowly, firmly down. She gasped for breath and quivered within his arms.

The telephone rang, startling Julie back to reality, as her brief time with Jack faded like sun-kissed fog. Would the pain of missing him fade as well?

"Hey, Terry, what's up?"

"Tomorrow's rehearsal has been canceled."

"Why? Has hell frozen?"

"You are the fourteenth person to ask me that. You people all think you're so original."

"Sorry. But when was the last time a rehearsal got canceled? Anytime this century? What gives?"

"The air conditioning system had a blowout and needs to be repaired. Powell Hall is sweltering. It's bad for the instruments, not to mention the people who play them. The pianos will certainly have to be tuned once the system is functioning. They estimate it will take most of the day, so we're doubling up for a morning and evening rehearsal the next day. Sorry, but the concerts begin right after that."

"I know, I know, and we have to have four rehearsals, whether we need them or not." Julie was not as put out as she led Terry to believe. She needed more practice time at home to be ready for these performances and today had been a waste as far as practicing went.

"Can't help it, Jules, The Hall is too hot to work in without air. Anything changes, I'll let you know." Terry's usual grumpy mood was not improved by the air conditioning situation.

They hung up, and Julie, relieved, went upstairs to her bedroom.

She stood outside on the balcony as she had the night before, pondering the past year of her life. So much had happened. Too many things had changed in too short a time. She closed her eyes and listened to the night music playing through the woods. Nature did not need four rehearsals, yet her evening sounds were lovely. There was a perfectly blended harmony ringing through the air with a hypnotic rhythm, following an invisible, yet palpably present conductor. Julie opened her eyes and stared into the vast woods. She thought of Pastor Grady's words. *Take a step of faith and trust that God knows what is best for you.*

She listened as God conducted the night symphony. Could God conduct her life as beautifully and intricately as this?

Closing the balcony doors, she undressed, slipped into her nightgown and climbed into bed. Although she was bone tired, her mind was restless and she lay in bed unable to unwind. She needed to concentrate on her music. Her music would get her through whatever it was that was going on; the craziness, the stress, her renewed sense of loss and emptiness. Her music was her life and without it she would be lost. Her mind drifted back in time, to that awful point in her childhood, the terrible tragedy that unwittingly launched her into undertaking what would become a successful career...

They had all gone to the lake for summer vacation; Mother, Daddy, Julie, Philip, Miyso, Su Li and Wanh. Julie was twelve years old that summer. Anne Creighton would never go out on the boat. She was deathly afraid of water and hated every summer at the lake. She tolerated this one week a year for everyone else's sake and because John took the family anywhere Anne chose over the Christmas holiday. But she was not a swimmer and was absolutely phobic about boating. John had insisted that his children have swimming lessons before they started kindergarten, and Julie and Philip were accomplished swimmers for their age. But swimming, boating, and anything else water related, were not activities in which Anne would participate.

The children were excited about going boating with John the following morning. Wanh was still too young, but the other three could hardly sleep. However, when morning came, it greeted Su Li with a high fever, so she stayed at the cabin with Anne and her mother, Miyso to care for her and Wanh. Dr. Creighton, after diagnosing the disappointed Su Li with nothing more than something viral, but still requiring rest and fluids, set off early with his children. It was a beautiful day, perfect for sailing and a little fishing. Anything he caught would be deliciously prepared by Miyso's capable hands.

Julie and Philip were delighted to spend time on the boat with their Daddy. At home, he was such a busy man with all of his patients to care for, but on vacation, they treasured their time with him. Vacations were family only, which of course, included the Tuans. The Creightons took two vacations each year. One week in the summer at the lake, and ten days in the winter wherever Mother wanted to go. Vacations meant laughing, eating out, sleeping in, and laughing some more. Daddy never wore a suit on vacations and rolled around on the floor with Julie, Philip, Su Li and Wanh, losing every wrestling match to the over-zealous munchkins. Even Miyso would laugh, although she often mentioned how much she missed her husband and wished he could have been with them to enjoy this kind of relaxation and fun.

Daddy was charting his course and Julie and Philip were on the deck looking for sharks.

"There are no sharks, Philip. This is a lake. Sharks are only in the oceans." But just to be sure, Julie scanned the water below them with great care.

"You don't know everything. There could be sharks. Someone could have flushed them down the toilets like the pet alligators that grow up in the sewers and eat people."

Julie rolled her eyes. Little brothers!

At last, there was no sign of land anywhere. Dr. Creighton began to teach his children the fine art of fishing in a perfect lake on a perfect day. Soon, the talk of man-eating sharks, alligators, and other creatures lurking in the sewers, plumbing lines and waterways, was forgotten and replaced with careful instructions for reeling in *the big one*. Both children gleefully listened with rapt attention. As far as Julie knew, nobody had ever reeled in the big one, but the day was so beautiful, the water so perfect, that maybe this would be the day the big one would be caught. Daddy was always so much fun on vacations! They sailed on until Daddy determined the perfect place to fish.

The three of them sat on the deck of the boat, lounging in their canvas recliners with their fishing lines in the water, relishing the blue skies, the peaceful quiet, and the lazy rocking of the boat, as the gentle waves lulled them into a hypnotic state of relaxation. Philip squirmed uncomfortably within the restraints of his life jacket and loosened the straps. Once comfortable, he, too, succumbed to the calm serenity of the boat's rhythmic rocking and began to nod off to sleep.

With no warning, the sky suddenly blackened and huge storm clouds appeared, blocking out the sun. The air quickly became cold and the waves grew rough and choppy, rocking the small yacht precariously. The unexpected storm moved in rapidly, tossing the boat in every direction. Dr. Creighton, alarmed by the abrupt change in weather, ordered his children below to safety.

"Julie! Take Philip and go below and wait. Stay with him. I'm heading us back. This looks to be a dangerous squall." He had no sooner spoken when the fast approaching storm hit with terrible force. The boat pitched and lurched uncontrollably. The gale blew water onto the deck. It stung Julie's face like sharp bullets of glass. Her eyes widened with fear. She reached for her brother's hand, but he was blown further from her.

"Philip, come back!" She ran after him, but by now the wind was so violent it tossed the little yacht as if it were a child's toy. Julie lost her balance and fell to the deck. Struggling to right herself and reach her brother, she noticed his life jacket was hanging loosely on him. Her fear intensified. "Philip!"

She ran toward him. The boat was battered by relentless winds. The waves crashed on the deck. The wood beneath them creaked and groaned, as if the weight of the three fragile humans on it was too much to bear. She just reached her brother when the boat cracked down the middle and shattered, throwing all three of them into the cold, turbulent water.

"Julie!" She heard her father yelling through the storm. "Hang on to Philip! Grab a piece of the boat and hold on to him!"

"Daddy! *Daddy!*" Julie cried, terrified. He was being carried away from them by the waves. A piece of the hull smacked into her shoulder blade and she turned around to grab it and hang on. Philip was almost close enough for her to touch. Their life jackets were drenched. She yelled to her brother as loudly as she could. "Philip! Grab the wood!" Somehow, he managed to do this and with all of her twelve-year-old strength, Julie maneuvered her body over the wood to hold on to him. The last thing she heard her father scream was, "Don't let go of Philip!"

The waves were fierce and furious, but Julie hung on to her brother with determined tenacity. They were both shivering from cold and fear. Julie had swallowed several mouthfuls of water. Horror-stricken, she realized she could neither see nor hear her father any longer. Julie and Philip were alone in the middle of the water, hanging on to each other over a piece of their boat while the storm raged violently over them, threatening to separate the siblings with wave after wave of terrifying force. Julie's arms ached. Her fingers dug into Philip until they were numb. Her teeth chattered and her shoulder throbbed from where the piece of the hull hit her. Her whole body hurt. How much longer could she hold on to Philip? Would anybody know to look for them?

The storm subsided as quickly as it had arisen and the sky returned to blue. Back at the cabin, Anne and Miyso had seen the black clouds over the lake. Anne tried to raise her husband on the radio, but after the third futile attempt, she called Lake Rescue Service in a panic. A rescue boat was dispatched to search for the Creightons.

How long had they been in the water, Julie wondered. It felt like hours. Could it have been days? Her eyes were getting heavy. She was more tired than she had ever been and struggled to stay awake. Her frail arms were too weak to hold on to Philip much longer. Although the storm had calmed, the waves were still choppy. Where was Daddy? Her head felt woozy and she wanted to go to sleep. She could no longer feel her legs. Maybe there were sharks after all, or maybe there was something else that had eaten her legs off. She didn't even care anymore.

Philip was ghastly white. "I'm tired, Julie. I can't hold on anymore." His voice was a breathless whisper, his eyelids swollen from water and fatigue. His lips were blue and his face was pale and ashen.

"You have to hold on, Philip, you have to. I can't do this much longer." Julie thought her voice sounded strange, like drunk people in the movies. The words all slurred together. Her arms were numb. Her muscles burned like fire from her shoulders to her fingers as she held on to her brother through sheer force of will. But her strength was gone. *Daddy, Daddy. I'm trying to hold on to Philip, but I can't. Daddy, help me. I can't hold on any longer. My arms are on fire.*

"I'm tired, Julie. I wanna go to sleep." There was no longer any fear in Philip's tiny voice. Julie tried to summon one last ounce of strength, but her reserve was gone. Exhaustion overcame her and she slowly released her grip. She watched Philip slip away and disappear under the water, his dark hair floating on the surface for a moment, like a spider with many legs. It was the last she saw of her well-loved brother.

"I love you, Philip," she wept, before she, too, finally surrendered to the fatigue that enveloped her small, battered body.

Julie knew nothing more after that, never felt the strong arms that pulled her into the rescue boat. As she lay on a hard surface, muffled voices floated over her head, but she couldn't quite hear them. She neither understood nor cared what they were saying. She thought she heard her father, only he was sobbing. But it couldn't be her Daddy. Her Daddy never cried. She drifted off to sleep.

She awoke in a hospital bed and found Miyso standing over her, lightly petting her head, worry etched on her small face. "You are better, now, Julie. I take you home and care for you. We have been much worry about you."

"Where's Philip? Where's Daddy?" she asked weakly. She thought her voice sounded far away, and she struggled to sit up. Miyso gave her a glass of water and her head began to clear.

"Come now, Julie. Put clothes on. I take you home."

They got into a taxi with Su Li and Wanh, but instead of going to the cabin, they drove to the airport. "Where are we going, Miyso?"

"Home, Julie. You have been sleep for many days. Doctor says you may go home for care. You be better soon."

"Where's Mom and Daddy? Where is Philip?" Julie asked, terribly confused. Miyso, a quiet woman of few words, was unusually silent now.

"They went home for Philip's funeral," Su Li volunteered helpfully.

Miyso sharply reprimanded her six-year old daughter, but Julie felt the full blow of Su Li's words. *I let go of Philip. I killed him. All I needed to do was hang on a little while longer, but I let him go.* Hot tears burned her face, as she cried silently the entire flight home, overcome with sorrow and guilt.

Anne and John met her at the airport with a subdued welcome. Although grateful to have their daughter back, they were grief-stricken at the loss of Philip. His body was discovered the day following the storm, and with Julie unconscious for who knew how long, they made the difficult decision to return home for Philip's funeral.

There was a distance between Julie and her father that Julie did not understand. She had thought he was dead. Wasn't he happy to have her back, safe and alive? *He blames me. I should have died, not Philip. This is my fault. That's why he doesn't talk to me. He knows I let go of Philip and that's why he died.*

Julie stayed in her room the remainder of the summer with Su Li constantly at her side. She wanted to talk to her parents about Philip, about how much she missed him and how very, very sorry she was that she could not hold on to him any longer, that she tried her very best. But her parents were too overcome with their own grief to help Julie deal with hers.

Miyso came in and sat on Julie's bed, next to her. "Julie, give your parents some time. They love you very much, but also miss Philip. They were much worry about you when you not wake up. I know you love your brother and try hard to save him, but too much for a little girl. Is big man's job, not job for little child. Your father try to reach both of you but was swept away. Rescue men find him first. Too late for Philip. Almost too late for you. Parents care very much for you. Just need time."

Julie knew Miyso was trying to help, trying to provide some measure of comfort, but her misery would not go away.

Su Li held Julie's hand after Miyso left. "Julie, play your cello. I miss your music." Although Julie felt too empty inside to play her cello, she picked it up anyway, just to please Su Li. She played the pieces she knew by heart, and then got out her books and began working through them.

Soon, she was practicing several hours each day. The only catharsis she could find was to lose herself in her music. By the end of summer, she had begun to heal, although loneliness and feelings of guilt still caused her heart to ache. The constant practicing resulted in Julie becoming quite an accomplished cellist for a twelve year old. Upon returning to school in September, she was happy that Miss Marshall, after two weeks of instrumental music, made arrangements for Julie to spend two days per week playing cello with the high school orchestra.

"She's holding back, Sam."

"Maybe she thinks that whatever it is, is unimportant."

"I think somebody's been bewitched by a pretty face and a pair of beautiful blue eyes, if you ask me. Sam, your objectivity, please!"

"Joe, it's been a long day. These are the things that were in his pockets. The ink pens are just ink pens. The business cards check out. Everything is just what it appears to be."

"What do you make of the pencil marks on the symphony itinerary?"

"I know, I know. Key cities in Europe. But I don't see how it all fits in. All I know is that she's not a part of it."

"What about Su Li? Have you located her in California? How does she check out?"

"Not yet. The break-in took me by surprise. I wasn't expecting to deal with that."

"If she suspects anything, she could have orchestrated it to throw off suspicion."

"I don't think so, Joe. I don't think there's any way she would drug her own dog."

"I don't think there's any way she would *kill* her own dog, but whatever he was given, he made a full recovery. How can you find that not suspicious?"

Sam let the remark go unchallenged. He and Joe had always made a good team. He didn't want an argument over something he was not even positive of to jeopardize their friendship or working relationship. "I'll check into Su Li tomorrow and let you know what I find out."

10

The waves were crashing over her head. She was going to drown. No use fighting something so much more powerful than you. She was gasping, now, struggling to keep her head above water. But the water kept coming and each new wave carried more and more of her strength away from her until soon, nothing would be left of her...

Julie woke up with a start, sweat drenching her nightgown. Her heartbeat was rapid and she was breathing hard. It had been more than ten years since she'd had this nightmare, but it had returned, every detail exact and graphic, just like when she was a child. What time was it? Too upset to go back to sleep, Julie remembered that tomorrow there would be two rehearsals; one at 11:00 a.m. and the other at 6:00 p.m. She had wasted this day without practice. She couldn't sleep anyway, so she went downstairs to the music room to finally practice. *The music room!* Julie had been so rattled by the break-in, she had not checked there, she supposed, because she didn't want the police going in there. Her music room may have been her private sanctuary, but of course, an intruder would have never respected that. *How could I have thought differently?*

Upon opening the door, she checked to see if anything had been touched by her unwelcome visitor. She turned on the light and carefully examined the entire room. Since the music room was so sparsely furnished, containing little else besides her instruments and music, she imagined nobody would have had much interest in here. However, this room, too, had been thoroughly searched. Again, although the intruder had been careful not to disturb or change anything, Julie could still tell that her things had been touched. This was *her* room, *her* sanctuary. Nobody was allowed in here. The music room was hers and hers alone. The thought of someone being here made her feel further violated and upset her even more.

She had not been this upset since she had found Jack in here, uninvited and unwelcome. It was the only time she had ever been truly angry with him. Even now, remembering the incident, she felt pangs of guilt at her outburst. She had put her room, her things, and herself before her husband. At the time, she had been furious, but with Jack dead, her anger now only seemed futile.

She had been out to lunch with Meg and returned earlier than she had planned. With Jack at work, Julie had decided to spend the afternoon practicing. But when she opened the door, she found Jack in the music room, looking guilt-stricken at her arrival. She was upset to see him there in the first place, but became enraged when she saw him holding in his hand, her most loved bow, broken in half.

"What do you think you're doing in here?" she had screeched at him. "Look at my bow! My favorite bow! You've destroyed my favorite bow! How dare you! How could you do this!" She had raged out of control and didn't care. He had no right to be in here, to touch her things and then break her bow.

Jack had seemed so penitent, as upset with himself as Julie was. "Darling, it was an accident. I am terribly sorry to have upset you. I was only admiring your tools of trade. I feel terrible, just terrible. I had no idea it would break like this. Sweetheart, you have two bows. Just use the other until I can replace this one."

"I don't like the other one as well. Jack, you had no right. *No right*! I can't believe you did this!" Julie had not been in a forgiving mood.

"Julie, love, please forgive me. I was out of line to have come in here and had I known this would happen, I never would have...oh please, Julie, please don't be so angry. I'll make it right. I promise."

But Julie would have none of it. This had been completely uncharacteristic of Jack. He had never made her angry before. No matter how long or sincerely he apologized, she remained unmoved. With rejection and regret all over his face, Jack finally left her alone.

The next few days in the Davenport home had been chilly and silent. Julie refused to speak to him and gave him a wide berth if he passed her in the hallways, staring coldly in front of her with her jaws clenched. One evening, Jack did not return at his usual 5:30 p.m. time. When an hour had gone by, Julie began to worry that either something had happened to him, or he had left her because of her refusal to forgive him. Guilt crept in, and with it, worry.

Please God, don't let anything happen to him. I've been horrible to him. He's the most wonderful man in the world. Please bring him back to me. I'll do anything. I can't live without him. As she was in the middle of promising to be a better wife, Jack walked in carrying a long box covered in gift wrap and chocolate roses. Julie ran to him and threw her arms around him, crying, and apologizing for her behavior, relieved that he was alive and home.

"No, Julie, I was wrong, but I am glad you are no longer angry with me. Now here. I have something special for you."

"Chocolate always works," she sniffed, wiping her tears away and unwrapping the chocolate flowers.

"The chocolate is part of the wrapping, darling. Open the box."

"Unless the box contains more chocolate, I am perfectly happy with the wrapping."

"Just open the box, Julie. And don't talk with your mouth full."

Inside the box was the most beautiful bow Julie had ever seen. She tenderly picked it up. In her hand it felt alive, light and pliant. She could not detect a name on it telling her the maker of the bow. Could it be a Peccatee? The balance was perfect. Cramming another chocolate in her mouth, she hurried to her music room, took out her cello and began to play with her new bow. The bow was spiccy, full of life as she drew it across the strings, commanding a beautiful, rich tone from her instrument. This bow felt as though it had been made especially for her, for her hand, her style. She was as excited as a child at Christmas. Setting her cello down, she ran to Jack, who stood in the doorway of the music room, not daring to enter.

"Thank you so much! I love it! Where did you get such a bow?"

"And I love you. Don't ask so many questions." He held her tightly and kissed her long and hard. It was the end of the only fight they ever had.

The whole intruder business had her puzzled. Somebody breaks in, searches the entire house, including the flour canister, takes great pains not to have the break-in discovered, and takes nothing that Julie could ascertain. They drug the dog, she supposed, in the hopes it would wear off without having been discovered, and then destroy the interior of Jack's car as if in a rage. None of it made sense.

Julie was a jumble of confusion and mixed emotions, but knew she would soon need to go back to sleep. To get up at this hour would only give her a short burst of energy, so she had best make good use of it since tomorrow's rehearsal schedule would be grueling. She worked for three hours on the "Back to Bach" music before returning to bed.

11

The next day went much as Julie expected. It felt good, however, to concentrate on something besides the craziness that had become her life the last few days.

After rehearsal, Julie decided to return to her old neighborhood to enjoy a light dinner. Although she could not bring herself to revisit Duff's, the place where Jack had followed her that first night, the Central West End was home to plenty of other great restaurants she liked. The evening was beautiful, slightly cool for summer, and the thought of enjoying a sandwich, salad and lemonade at an outdoor table in her bustling former neighborhood was too inviting to pass up. Besides, this was her favorite place to people watch.

Julie, however, was not the only person in St. Louis with the same idea. Even though it was past dinnertime, the Central West End was buzzing with activity. When she brought her tray outside to find a table, Julie was dismayed to find all the tables full. Just as she was turning around to eat inside, she heard someone call her name.

She could barely suppress a surprised smile when she saw Detective Sam Hernandez beckoning her over to his table. He seemed delighted to see her and brushed off a chair for her to sit down.

"You eating alone, too? Kind of far from home, aren't you?"

"We had a double rehearsal today. Yesterday's was canceled due to technical difficulties, specifically, no air conditioning, so we had to make up the missed rehearsal. In the SLSO, our slogan is four rehearsals, whether we need them or not. Speaking of far from home, don't tell me you live down here and go to Pineview to be a cop."

Sam smiled at her. "No. I had to testify in court downtown this afternoon, and decided while I was in town to run a few errands and grab a bite. I see we have the same good taste in food. I like this part of town for good eats."

"Yeah, I used to live only a couple of blocks from here. I know all the good places to eat in the Central West End. And there are plenty of them. It's not like Pineview has any decent restaurants, you know. Of course, home is always the best place, but it's too late tonight." *Home is always the best place when Su Li is there, anyway.*

"Oh yeah? You a good cook?"

Something similar to déjà vu washed over Julie. She decided to try the honest approach this time, for a change, especially with a cop. Especially with a cop who thought she was some sort of a suspect.

"Actually, my cooking is dreadful beyond description. I could have given lessons to Lucrezia Borgia." She started laughing and began recounting her culinary disasters. "I pour a pretty mean bowl of Cocoa Puffs," she confessed.

"So Su Li cooks while Julie fiddles, something like that? How did you meet her? She wasn't there either time I was at your home."

"Awfully corny, Detective Hernandez," she groaned.

"Sam. Please call me Sam."

He was refreshingly easy to talk to. Julie realized it had been a long time since she had talked with someone other than Su Li or Meg, and she was lonelier than she had been willing to admit. She told him about her childhood, Su Li and Miyso, Philip, the symphony, how she met Jack, even her struggles to manage her grief, but she held back about being followed, the phone calls, and her increasing fear and confusion over these recent events.

Suddenly, she felt self-conscious and embarrassed. "I, ah, I'm afraid I've been doing all the talking," she stammered. "I don't know anything about you."

"I live alone. My wife and I divorced two years ago."

"I'm sorry."

"We had no children, so at least there were no small lives to mess up. It was too hard for her to be married to a man in my profession. I did not handle stress very well. She did not handle the danger in my work very well. I kept everything bottled up inside. After a while, we stopped talking. We eventually became strangers in the same house. The divorce was amicable enough. We didn't have much. We were both working and made about the same money. She remarried earlier this year. We're not in touch. There's not really much to tell. In my line of work there's a pretty high divorce rate."

Julie felt herself being drawn to Sam. He was kind and soft spoken. She believed he was hurting and dealing with his own struggles; his pain was just a different type than hers. She didn't know what to say to him, so she said nothing, feeling awkward.

"Julie," Sam broke the silence. "It is getting quite late. And if I understood you correctly, you have a concert tomorrow. I have enjoyed your company immensely, but even the Central West End denizens are going to bed. Why don't I see you to your car?"

12

The phone woke a groggy, disoriented Julie.

"Good morning, princess. It's after ten. Rough night?"

"Hi, Meg. After ten! Meg, I gotta go. We have a concert at two and another at six. What's up? Make it quick."

"Yes, your highness. Just checking in on you. Anything to report?"

"No, I'm fine. I gotta get ready."

"Okay, okay. Got it. Bye."

Ten o'clock! How could I sleep so long?

She threw on shorts and a t-shirt and took Fred for a quick, productive walk.

In the shower, Julie reflected on last night. It was a pleasant coincidence running into Sam. She enjoyed their conversation, seeing him less as a cop and more as a man. Sam was quiet and friendly. He was so different from Jack. Now why would a thought like that come to mind? Because she found him attractive? Because she found herself drawn to him and that made her feel, what? Guilty? Unfaithful? Human?

"This is a really bad idea," she mumbled to the mirror as she applied her make-up. "I'm at the top of his list of suspects for starters." She stopped short. Sinking down heavily onto her bed, Julie sighed, near tears. *He was pumping me for information. For all I know, last night was no coincidence. No, that's wrong.*

There were a million things he could have asked me that he didn't. But I really did all the talking. He said next to nothing, while I told him nearly everything about myself. His questions and prodding were so gently executed. Was he just doing his job, or is he really interested in me? We seemed to enjoy each other's company. I know we did. He's too genuine. I shouldn't be so untrusting. Should I?

"What you should be doing is finishing your face and getting ready for this performance," the face in the mirror said back.

Joe Spence listened for the fourth time to the conversation played by Sam describing the break-in at Julie's house.

"We're all after the same thing. What I don't understand is why would the perp go to the trouble of trying to cover up his actions in the house while destroying the Jaguar? It doesn't make sense. Stealthy and secretive in the house, yet, in the car, personal and passionate, full of rage. How does *that* add up? Another thing. She was adamant that those windows were all locked, yet the investigating officer found the one window unlocked."

"Joe, you should see this place. There must be dozens of windows. It's got to be the most expensive digs in Pineview. All glass and cedar and stone. With the weather being cooler than normal, she probably had some fresh air coming in. It's easy enough to believe she didn't have all the windows locked."

"Let's look at this objectively, Sam. Pineview is out in the middle of nowhere. Pineview's idea of a crime wave is a bar fight, a dog bite and a little teenage vandalism, all in one week. This lady lives in the middle of nowhere in a town that's located in the middle of nowhere. I'm willing to bet that half of those people probably figure their windows are locked, not that it would matter, but they wouldn't be so stomp-your-foot adamant about it. Now, unless Ms. Davenport is involved in something that requires her home to be locked up tightly, then how is it that she is so sure-fire certain that every single one of those dozens of windows was locked?"

"Maybe she's afraid of something. Or someone."

"Very astute," Joe replied with exaggerated sarcasm.

"I don't mean because she's guilty. Maybe she's being threatened. I don't know."

"You still think she's holding back information?"

Sam sighed audibly. "I think she's holding back something. That doesn't mean it's pertinent information."

"Did you know she went out to McGarret's airfield?"

"Yeah, yeah, I know. She hasn't mentioned it."

"There's been no sign of Russ Richards, the only mechanic Jack Davenport allowed to work on his plane. Guy just vanishes. Last seen the day Davenport took off on his last flight. Not listed as a passenger, not that he would have been one. Davenport always flew alone. All we know about Richards is that he is a top-flight mechanic with an alcohol problem. He's now officially missing. And Julie was asking about him."

"That doesn't mean she knows something. I don't think she found anything out. Joe, what do you expect her to do? I dropped a huge bombshell on her that her husband's *accident*, for lack of a better word, was suspicious. What do you expect her to do? Say, 'Oh, okay. Would you care for some crumpets with your tea?' Maybe she just wanted to hear her husband's mechanic say he was certain the plane was in good working condition. She probably has a lot of questions herself that she wants answered."

"Or she's paying for somebody's silence."

Julie pulled her white Maxima onto eastbound Highway 44 for the long drive to Grand Avenue, her cello securely strapped in the back seat. Sitting on the westbound exit ramp on the other side of the highway, a green Buick jumped to life and made its way down the winding road that would eventually lead to the Davenport home. Manny Tupelo smiled to himself as the Maxima's tail lights disappeared in his rear view window. Now, he would have all kinds of time to find what he was looking for. Julie would be out of the house for several hours, providing him every opportunity he needed to get what he wanted. Nothing would stop him now.

"Are you certain she does not know you were in the house?" the captain asked.

"I left no trace at all. I even drugged the dog."

The captain nodded his approval. Killing the dog would have raised all kinds of alarms unnecessarily. By drugging him, the effects would have worn off by the time the Davenport woman got home, and she would have simply thought he was not such a good watch dog after all. The captain was pleased. "Did you have enough time to go through the car?"

"Yes. I searched the house first, in case the drug wore off on the dog and also because it would be easy to hear her coming in from the garage and I would have time to get away back through the woods. She would be none the wiser."

"Yet still, you come up empty handed."

"I am not finished, sir. Not yet. I am beginning to believe that Julie Davenport is expendable. However, I have one more idea."

The captain raised one eyebrow in doubt, but leaned forward to huddle with his top agent to listen to yet another idea.

The first concert was uneventful. Afternoon audiences tended to be smaller and less enthusiastic than their evening counterparts. Julie knew better than to expect anything more than polite applause. As soon as the concert was over, Julie left to grab a quick bite of early dinner at a nearby diner. She didn't like to eat before a performance, but when the symphony had both afternoon and evening concerts, she couldn't hold out that many hours on an empty stomach. She returned to The Hall for the second performance, feeling tired, fidgety and nervous, bothered by thoughts that she should be home. When it was time for the orchestra members to make their entrance onto the stage, Julie felt herself distracted and inattentive.

The second concert was going well enough, even though Julie was having a difficult time concentrating. Her stand partner threw her a couple of questioning looks which she ignored, but accepted as a warning to pay closer attention. She avoided him at intermission. For that matter, she avoided everyone. She decided to tell Sam all that had happened. If he knew everything that was going on, maybe he could help. The more she thought about it, the more she decided Sam could be trusted.

The second half of the concert seemed to drag on forever, but it finally ended with the audience leaping to a standing ovation. That was always gratifying. The audiences they played to in St. Louis were sophisticated, knowledgeable, and appreciative of the fine performances the St. Louis Symphony Orchestra turned out routinely. They expressed their appreciation with thunderous and prolonged applause. Julie loved the way their music could touch the hearts of people, but her own heart was not in this evening's performance and she felt like a cheater standing up with the rest of the orchestra to accept the applause. She left as quickly as possible to begin her drive home.

She turned into her driveway, unaware of the green Buick parked off the road less than a quarter of a mile past her driveway, hidden within a grove of trees.

"Oh, no!" Julie exclaimed out loud. "I forgot to pick up dog food!" *Dumb, dumb, dumb.* She drove around to the front of the house under the canopy so she could run in quickly, drop off her cello and change from her concert clothes to jeans before going out again to the feed store. She needed to hurry, as the feed store would be closing soon. She removed her cello from the back seat and entered the house through the front door. The house was eerily silent and Julie immediately sensed something was wrong. She set her cello down in the spacious foyer. The house was too quiet, the stillness charged with a silent, unnamed danger. Her heart began to race.

She flipped the light switch, but the house remained dark. She felt goose bumps tingling on her skin as she hurried from the foyer into the living room and flipped the light switch. Nothing. Same in the dining room. Panic rising in her throat, her trembling fingers fumbled for the lamp switch in the hallway. No light. Only darkness. And eerie silence.

She tried to call for Fred, but just as no current coursed through the house, neither did sound come from her throat. Where was he? She was not alone in the house. She sensed the presence of another person, but did not know where he was. Terror gripped her, swelling in her stomach and filling her trembling body with tension. She wanted to run, but her shoes were heavy as cement. She stood glued to the floor, frozen in fear. The palpable presence of danger crept through her like a viper weaving its path toward its trembling prey. She had to find Fred…and the cats.

Willing herself to move, she stepped gingerly into the kitchen, engulfed in the silent darkness. The kitchen swallowed her like a black hole, empty, menacing and deadly still. She stood noiselessly, her eyes straining to adjust to the dark, her pulse racing. Behind her, the silence was broken as Julie heard a sharp click, the blade of a buck knife locking into place. She gasped and instinctively lurched forward, but a strong hand grabbed her hair and with a violent yank, she was pulled back and held against a sweaty man whose breathing was almost as hard and fast as her own. He held the knife against her throat and pressed. "I want that list," he hissed into her ear. Not surprisingly, she recognized his voice.

Scratching. Julie heard scratching coming from the door in the kitchen that led to the basement. Fred! He was whining and barking now. He knew she was home and in trouble. *Get to the door. I have to get to the door. I have to let Fred out of the basement.*

The man briefly let go of her hair to grab her arm. In that split second, Julie lunged for the basement door, flinging it open to an angry, snarling Fred. Fred charged into the kitchen after the intruder, who was already running for the front door, but Fred was faster. He leapt onto the man's back, ripping his throat with his teeth, growling viciously and hanging on with a tenacious grip. Dog and man rolled together, each locked in a struggle for victory.

The man, fighting for his life, took his knife, slashed at the dog's chest, and the huge shepherd howled in pain, collapsing in a heap onto the rug in the foyer, his blood flowing from him and pooling onto the rug.

Julie screamed in terror as the man, covered in his own blood, mingled with Fred's, stood unsteadily and walked toward her, wielding the knife. She held her arms up protectively as he slashed wildly at her, feeling the sting of her flesh being cut. They were struggling at the bottom of the staircase when Johann and timid little Sebastienne flew down the stairs, deftly jumping on Julie's attacker, clawing the man's face and eyes, a hissing flurry of black and orange fur. Overcome, the man dropped the knife and ran out the front door.

Julie, choking and gasping for air, felt hot tears streaming down her face as she stumbled over to Fred, lying motionless on the rug. He was still breathing and as Julie reached for him, he wagged his tail weakly. "Hang in there, Fred. Stay with me, boy, stay with me." Julie pulled the rug that Fred was lying on slowly across the floor and out the front door, less than fifteen feet from where the Maxima was parked. He weighed 95 pounds, not much less than Julie. She opened the back door and taking the rug, wrapped it around Fred and hefted the dog onto the back seat, twisting her left ankle.

As she sped down her driveway, she picked up her car phone. The vet's number was on the phone's speed dial. The animal hospital was open late two nights a week. Julie prayed tonight was one of them.

Dr. Pam Medcalf was starting to lock the door to the animal hospital which she and her husband, also a veterinarian, owned, when she heard the phone ring. *It's forty minutes past closing time on a late night as it is. Let the answering machine get it.* Her husband was waiting for her in the car. They were both tired after a long and busy day and wanted to get home, put their feet up, and relax with a nice Pinot Noir a grateful patient had given them. Dr. Medcalf sighed. *What's one more call?* She motioned to her husband to wait a second and answered the phone to a woman crying hysterically. She understood the words, Fred, stabbed, and on my way.

"Julie Davenport? Is that you?"

Choked sobs confirmed that it was.

"Mark and I will wait right here for you. Get here as quickly as you can." As if Julie needed to be told. Pam motioned for Mark to come in, and they began to prep for surgery.

Julie drove faster than she ever had in her life, feeling the Maxima leave the ground as she flew over the hills, rounding the curves at breakneck speed.

She never noticed the green Buick overturned off the side of the road as she sped past it. In the driver's seat, covered with bites and claw marks from three protective pets, slumped over, lay the blood-smeared body of Manny Tupelo with a bullet through his head.

Two miles from the animal hospital, a squad car was parked, patiently waiting for a speeder to give the bored officer something to do on this quiet evening in Pineview. Julie's white blur streaking by did not disappoint him. He turned on his lights and siren, but the white Maxima did not slow in the least, so he called in the license number while he continued in hot pursuit. A second squad car heard the call and joined in the chase.

Julie neither slowed nor stopped until she reached the front of the vet's office where Mark and Pam were waiting, the operating room already prepared. They hurried the dog into the hospital, still lying on the rug, as two squad cars pulled in behind Julie, who had run into the hospital behind the Medcalfs. The officers winced at the sight of the beautiful, badly injured German Shepherd. If this had been a K-9 officer and dog, they would have done the same thing as this woman.

The officers approached Julie, who was covered with blood and hysterical. She dropped her head into her hands and sobbed uncontrollably, her shoulders shaking as she gulped and heaved air between fresh tears. The officers then noted the bloody gashes on her arms and hands where she had been slashed fending off her attacker. She sat down heavily in a chair in the waiting room. This was not at all what they expected on a routine speeding violation.

Before they could speak to Julie, a grey sedan pulled in behind their squad cars and Sam Hernandez jumped out of his car. He spoke briefly and quietly to the policemen and they left.

He surveyed a blood-streaked Julie, noting the cuts and sat beside her. Her face was still buried in her hands. "Julie," he said softly. She looked up. "I sent the officers away. Suppose you tell me what happened tonight."

"He tried to kill me," she sobbed. "He tried to kill Fred. Fred might die." Julie was choking on her words. "I can't lose Fred. I can't lose him."

"Who is *he*, Julie? Tell me who this man is."

His voice was calm and soothing, comforting her. Sam was going to make everything better. *Just tell him and he will fix it.*

"Fred…" Julie started and began sobbing again.

"Fred is in good hands. They are doing all they can for him. Somebody hurt you tonight, Julie. You said he tried to kill you. I think it's time you tell me what's going on, don't you?"

"The man who was following me. The man who keeps calling me." Julie had turned white and began to shake.

Sam debated the wisdom of continuing his questioning and decided it was more important to get Julie to a hospital. Her cuts needed attention, and although he suspected much of the blood on her belonged to her dog, he needed to be cautious. Her ghostly color concerned him.

"Julie, I want to take you to the hospital. Will you let me drive you? I think it would be best if you were seen by a doctor." Sam's voice was low and gentle.

"What about Fred? I can't leave him."

"Julie, you're going to have to leave him, anyway."

Julie and Sam started at the sound of Mark Medcalf's deep, solemn voice. Neither of them heard him enter the waiting room.

"How is Fred? Is he going to be okay?" She struggled to speak, her voice trembling and high pitched.

"Fred is still in surgery. It is going well so far, but he is not out of the woods, yet. He has lost a lot of blood, but you got him here quickly. When we are finished, Pam is going to stay here through the night while I go home to sleep for a few hours. When I come back, she will go home to sleep. Fred needs to be watched very carefully, Julie, but not by you. He needs someone who knows what to do if he has a crisis tonight. Now, let your friend take you to the hospital so you will be in good condition to care for Fred when he is strong enough to go home. I need to get back to him now. Call the office in the morning."

Dr. Medcalf spoke to her as though she was a child, but nobody seemed to object. He was unsure of how much she understood in her current state of mind.

Mark Medcalf returned to the operating room. "How is she?" his wife asked, still stitching her patient.

"I'm not too sure what all she was able to understand right now. She's in shock. Good thing she has a friend with her." They finished tending to Fred, and Mark kissed his wife goodnight before locking her in the clinic. "I'll see you in a few hours."

Julie allowed Sam to help her to his car. He carefully fastened the seat belt around her and drove to the emergency room.

Julie's cuts were deep enough to create a bloody mess, but thankfully, only required a few small stitches. It was expected that she would heal with no permanent scarring. Had her cuts been more severe, there might have been nerve damage which could have ended her career. The doctor voiced more concern for her emotional state than for her physical condition. Her cuts and bruises would be sore for several days, but she suffered no serious injuries. The nurses cleaned and bandaged her wounds. The doctor gave her a short-term antibiotic to prevent infection and a mild sedative and then released her into Sam's care.

By the time they got back into Sam's car, Julie was feeling a little better, and although all she wanted was to retreat into silence, she was capable of talking coherently. As they pulled out of the parking lot, she reached for Sam's hand.

"Thank you," she whispered. Sam took her hand, gently squeezed it and kept it enveloped in his hand. She left it there, placidly.

Oh, boy, this is trouble. By now, Sam believed Julie was exactly as she appeared; a sweet, naïve victim, confused and traumatized from the many recent events. However, he knew Joe was just as certain she was involved, if not the prime suspect. But out loud he asked her, "Julie, would you like to stop for coffee?" She nodded and he pulled into an all-night diner.

He helped her out of the car. She looked a mess, her white summer concert clothes ripped and stained with blood, her hair tangled and her tear-streaked face blotchy from stress and smeared make-up. Her arms were wrapped in white gauze bandages and her left ankle was wrapped in an ace bandage. Sam held his lips together tightly in an effort not to smile. For some reason, this dirty, little waiflike creature was absolutely beautiful to him. They entered the diner, looking quite the unusual pair. He was wearing his usual suit and tie and was completely unscathed. She looked as if she had just fought a war single handedly.

They sat in a corner booth, away from the curious stares of the few people in the diner at such a late hour and Sam ordered two coffees. He drank his black and watched as Julie poured sugar and cream into hers, stirring the stuff into oblivion. He asked her if she felt she could talk to him and she nodded. She looked completely defeated.

She told him all that had happened since the day she was followed home, the phone calls, the trip to McGarret's, everything. They stayed in the booth talking quietly for over an hour while the waitress filled Sam's cup several times.

Finally, Julie told Sam she was spent and asked to go home. Sam nodded and asked, "Aren't you going to finish your coffee?" She looked up at him and smiled wanly. "I don't like coffee."

Sam bit his lip to keep from smiling. "Come on, let's go." He resisted calling her, honey, although it was on the tip of his tongue. "I'll take you home."

"I need my car. I'm fine to drive."

Julie was anything but fine to drive and Sam would not hear of it. She was still in shock and under the sedative. He promised to pick her up first thing in the morning and take her to her car, but for now, he would see her safely home. Surprisingly, Julie did not argue with him. He knew that was not because she agreed with him, of course; she was simply out of steam. Besides, he wanted her to feel safe and secure.

He carefully buckled her into the passenger seat, avoiding her wrists, afraid of hurting her, and started the engine. Suddenly, Julie bolted upright.

"What's the matter?"

"I think I left the door unlocked. What if he comes back? What if the cats get out?"

"I think everything will be fine, Julie. But I promise you, I will go through every inch of that house before I leave." He would have done that whether she asked him to or not. "From what you've told me, I think your pets did quite a number on your attacker and I think he probably needs some medical attention himself tonight."

Sam did not tell her that her beloved pets would have to be quarantined for ten days, since they all drew blood. No need to further upset her.

As they turned off the highway exit onto the road, they passed the place where Manny Tupelo's car had been, the grass matted down and the bushes flattened.

"Looks like someone had an accident here tonight," Sam remarked.

"Yeah, people really drive crazy on these roads."

As they pulled into her driveway, they saw the front door standing open. Sam told Julie to stay in the car while he checked the house. Julie ignored him, of course, and followed behind, worried about Johann and Sebastienne.

"Didn't I just tell you to stay in the car?"

"This is *my* house. *My* cats. *My* nightmare. Am I under arrest?"

"No. Of course, not." *Not yet.*

"Then I'm going with you."

As they approached the open front door, Sam gently pushed Julie off to the side and pulled his gun out of his shoulder holster. Julie shuddered at the sight of it and briefly hesitated, as though rethinking her decision to go in with him. He turned on a small flashlight which provided little illumination. Sam forcefully kicked the door all the way open and they heard the twangy echo of her cello she had left in the foyer as it fell over. Julie cringed, and Sam hoped the hard shell case would offer adequate protection for her precious instrument.

The foyer appeared the same as when Julie left it. Blood spatters and streaks along the wall, mixed with piles of fur gave the foyer the appearance that Julie had redecorated with a voodoo theme. Scraps of material, some from her white concert dress, some from the clothing of her assailant, were scattered at the foot of the staircase. Julie stood motionless a moment, reliving the ordeal.

Sam continued his search, beginning in the living room.

"Holy—" He stopped short.

Julie came up behind him. She stepped into the living room and as her eyes adjusted to the dimly lit room, she caught her breath and stiffened. The sofa, the chairs, the drapes, everything was slashed. Lamps were broken, wall hangings torn down and cut open, glass and furniture stuffing were strewn all over the living room. Books were torn up and the carpet was gouged.

"Fire the housekeeper," he whispered drily to her. "Did your living room look like this when you came home earlier tonight?"

"No. Everything was in place," she whispered back. "Besides, I told you, Su Li, my housekeeper and best friend, don't forget, is out of town. You told me he wouldn't be back. What kind of a cop are you, anyway? Do you think he's still in the house?"

"Where is your fuse box? We need to get the lights back on."

"In the basement at the bottom of the stairs, on the wall to your immediate right. You have to go through the kitchen." She stopped and breathed deeply. "I don't think I can go into the kitchen." While the thought of being in a kitchen usually terrified her, this time, it was for different reasons than the usual. "I'll wait for you in the dining room."

Sam squeezed her hand. "I'll see to the fuse box. You wait here."

Soon the lights were on and Sam found Julie under the dining room table, cradling two nervous cats in her lap. Sam made certain the house was empty, but whoever had been here had destroyed the living room, the master bedroom, and the office.

Certain that they were alone in the house, they resumed talking normally. "Julie, it's nearly sunrise and you haven't slept."

"I can't sleep in this house. Not now, anyway. I'll get a hotel room."

"What about your cats?"

"Oh, yeah." Julie was so tired she was no longer capable of thinking clearly. "I'm tired and I'm scared. I don't know what I should do."

"Julie, you have other bedrooms. If you'd like, I'll stay in one and you can stay in one of the others."

At this point, Julie would have slept in a den of gorillas if it came with a pillow, so she meekly agreed. Sam took the bedroom next to hers.

13

"Terry, hi, this is Julie Davenport. I'm sorry, but I need to take a few days off. When I got home last night, my place had been burglarized and thoroughly trashed. It's a real mess. Probably kids on something, ya know? Anyway, it's gonna take me a while to clean this place up."

"Geez, Jules, who can even find your place? Wow, I'm real sorry to hear about that. Sure, take a few days, no problem. I hope they catch whoever did it."

Julie knew that in spite of Terry's crabby demeanor, he had a sympathetic heart. While he was known as a glass-half-empty grouch, he had shown Julie uncharacteristic kindness since Jack's accident.

She hated taking time off. The symphony had been very generous to her when Jack died, giving her a liberal extended leave of absence. Their vacation and sick leave policies were more than adequate and she did not want to take advantage. However, Julie was past the point where she could concentrate on music or anything, for that matter. She was trying to function on her last frayed nerve, without having to perform on top of it.

Removing her bandages, she carefully showered and dressed, applied fresh bandages, and followed her nose downstairs to the smell of breakfast cooking. She had slept late into the morning, but Sam was up early and had already made several phone calls.

"Hey, I thought for a minute Su Li was back. Good morning. Bacon and eggs. What a treat." She wanted to kiss him, but held back. That would have been inappropriate, even though she was deeply grateful for his protection and care. She vacillated on whether having Sam here overnight was a good idea. But she had been much too frightened to stay by herself and too overtired to think of anything else.

"Here, have some hot chocolate, since you can't start your day without a fix. Wish you had some coffee around here. I could really use some. Sleep well?"

"Like a rock, surprisingly. Thanks. Probably the sedative. I'm still feeling the after-effects. Mmmm. Good cocoa. Sorry about the coffee. Nobody here drinks it and I don't entertain very often. So, where do we go from here?"

"Julie, I have to go to work. I hate leaving you here. Do you have a friend you could stay with?"

"Meg. But I don't want to. It would be a real imposition on her. And then, of course, there's still the cats. Anyway, I have to start cleaning this mess, although, I hardly know where to begin. Su Li picked a terrible time to leave, but of course, with Miyso being terminal, there's never a good time for that. Oh, no. I feel so guilty for even thinking such a thing."

But Sam had that exact thought. He found it suspicious that as soon as Su Li left, hell arrived. However, further checking backed up what Julie told him about Su Li's mother dying of cancer. Every fact had to be checked and confirmed, but he had thought the Su Li angle was a long shot anyway, given the girls' lifelong history and close friendship. It was still incredible timing, and it occurred to Sam that someone close enough to Julie to know these circumstances may have been waiting for the right opportunity. Or, perhaps she was being watched and bugged by somebody else, which he feared was more likely. Whatever the case, somebody waited for Julie to be alone and vulnerable. Again, still too many loose ends. He had many pieces of a puzzle, but could not determine how they fit together.

"Julie, I need to have the crime crew here before you touch anything. They need to take photographs and collect evidence. Be sure you ask for ID, and please, *please,* do not touch anything until they have finished. Find a room that was not damaged and wait there until you are given the all clear. And speaking of cleaning up, there is a company the department uses to take care of crime scene cleanup. They do a good job. If you like, when the crime scene unit is finished, I can make a call and send the clean-up crew in for you."

"Oh, yeah, I'd like! Tackling this job is more than I even want to think about. But Sam, I need to check my cello and bow. They may have been damaged and I don't want to risk further damage. I won't touch anything else, okay?"

He agreed. He knew he was already in deep trouble for not calling in the events of last night when they first unfolded, and was trying to determine the best way to explain his actions without making a bad situation worse.

"You could even spend the day shopping for new furniture. I imagine your insurance company will cover most of this. I'm gonna have a uniform on the premises for a couple of days for your protection, at least until I can find out more about what's going on."

Julie opened her mouth, but Sam kept on talking, cutting her off.

"Don't bother arguing with me. You won't get anywhere." He served her breakfast. "By the way, I called the animal hospital. Fred is doing better. They want to keep him a few more days."

"I wanna go see him."

"The vets prefer that you don't. He is hooked to an IV and if he sees, smells, or hears you, he may become too excited and re-injure himself. I know you don't want to risk that. They are keeping him sedated. It's best that you just let him rest and heal. He'll be fine."

Sam turned away and busied himself cleaning the breakfast dishes before heading out to work.

Julie studied him. It was now her turn to look fresh and clean. He was rumpled and needed a shave. She guessed he had not slept much last night. She was having trouble remembering the details of everything that happened after the concert. Her memory was blurry. She attributed that to the last remnants of the sedative still needing to wear off. She did remember Sam holding her hand in the car. He made her feel warm and safe when she was with him.

He broke her reverie. "I gotta go. Stay locked in until the crime crew is finished and the cleaning crew arrives. Then you can go out for as long as you like. They're gonna be here a long time. Keep the cats put away, because the door may be left open for periods of time. Here's my card again. Call me if you need me for anything, got it? I've made arrangements for your car to be delivered here this morning. You left the keys in the ignition last night, so it's an easy fix. Remember, don't touch anything."

She walked him to the door. "Thank you for everything. I don't know how I could have managed any of this without you." She put her arms around him and hugged him. She felt his strong arms around her, pulling her tightly to his chest, holding her there. She could feel his heart beating almost as fast as hers. Then he released her.

"Just doing my job, ma'am." He smiled at her, tipping his imaginary cap, touched her face, and left.

Julie had calls to make, places to go, people to see. But first, she needed to check her cello. She took it into the music room and opened the case. The bridge and pegs were firmly in place and nothing appeared loose. After a careful visual inspection, she could detect no damage. She played it for a while and determined it had survived being hit by the door, but she would mention it to Arturo when she took her bow in to have the hair replaced next week. It was already overdue. Arturo had not seen the new bow that Jack had given her. She was looking forward to showing it to him.

She telephoned the insurance company, Dr. Medcalf, Arturo, Meg who was not home and finally, Su Li.

"Hey, Julie, I was going to call you tonight. How are things going on the home front?"

Just great, Su Li. Someone tried to kill me last night. They nearly succeeded in killing my dog. My house was trashed, my cats traumatized, my husband's plane accident was really a murder and I'm the prime suspect. And, today my home will be filled with strangers while I go out furniture shopping. I am attracted to a man who thinks I'm mixed up in something illegal, and I can't tell you any of this stuff, because you are clear across the country to be with your dying mother, whom I love as if she were my own. Other than that, it's the same ol', same ol'. "Everything's fine. How is Miyso?"

"She's doing badly. She sleeps most of the time, drug induced and when she is awake, she is not very much aware of her surroundings." Su Li's voice sounded tired and deflated. Julie longed to be with her, to comfort her and Wanh, to share their burden. Su Li had always been there for her, and now, Julie was half a country away from her during her time of need.

"I'm so sorry, Su Li. How are you and Wanh holding up?"

"Wanh has become silent and withdrawn. He does not share his thoughts and feelings. His suffering is his own. He is in much pain. I feel as though I am just existing. Numb is better than pain. My sleep is poor and I am trying to accept that I will soon lose my mother. I cannot get Wanh to talk about it."

"Do you need anything? Anything at all? Would you like me to come to California? I will be on the next plane, if you say the word."

"No. It would do no good. I know I have your prayers and support, but my mother has no hope. I would like to hear what is happening at home?"

Oh, I rather doubt that. "Well, I've been thinking about doing a little redecorating, you know, maybe some new furniture." *About as likely as wanting to try some new recipes.*

"Excuse me, is this Julie Davenport?" She sounded more like Su Li now. "Have you been sick? Your furniture is beautiful, and anyway, it's still new. Is there something you're not telling me?"

What was your first clue? "It's just that, you know, Jack picked out everything and I thought maybe it would be a good idea not to have so many reminders around." *Yeah, that sounds good.*

"Well, Julie, maybe that's a good idea. How are Johann, Sebastienne, and Fred? Do they miss me?"

"Of course they miss you. They're fine. Which reminds me, there's an awful lot of dog hair around here. Where is the vacuum?"

"Laundry room closet. First, you plug it in, then you flip the switch on the handle, and then you push it back and forth. Do you want to get a pen and write that down?"

"Nope. I think I can handle it. Thank you."

"I need to go now, Julie. And no, I don't need money or anything. At least, I don't need anything a person can provide. Only prayers. I miss you."

"I miss you, too, Su Li. Give my love to Wanh and Miyso."

Julie sighed heavily and trudged slowly into the hearth room. She pulled her chocolates out of the wall safe, debating which to choose. She was tempted to cram the whole box in her mouth at once, but thought better of it. She chose a solid, intensely dark chocolate. She inhaled deeply, breathing in the strong chocolate scent, letting it fill her olfactory senses before putting it into her mouth. It was very dark, rich, and slightly bitter, brimming with decadent cocoa. It was a perfect piece of ultra-dark chocolate, pure, unadulterated food of the gods. She leaned back in Jack's chair and closed her eyes. The chocolate melted slowly on her tongue, spilling over and slathering the inside of her mouth, a harmonious blend of sweet and bitter, bathing her senses in warm contentment...

He was behind her, now, rubbing her neck, her shoulders, massaging her temples, making the stress go away, making all of the bad things go away. He lifted the back of her hair and began kissing her neck tenderly, sweetly, sending shivers throughout her body.

He was unbuttoning her blouse, slow and steady, his lips moving over her face and neck. She smiled and leaned back into him, kissing him with her eyes closed. "Mmmm, Jack."

He came around to face her and was kissing her hard now, his passion building. She pressed her body close to his, reveling in the sensations he stirred within her. She opened her eyes to look into his eyes, deep and blue. Only, it was not Jack's face. It was Sam's.

Julie bolted upright, shocked at herself. How could she do this?

But before she could reprove herself further, she heard a noise in the driveway. Peeking out of what was left of the living room draperies, she saw that her car had been delivered. The crime crew was also arriving.

Good. She wanted to leave.

"Little late this morning, aren't you, Sam? I've been paging you for hours."

"Sorry, Joe. Rough night. What's up?"

"You're not the only one who's had a rough night. At least you're not Manny Tupelo."

"Who's Manny Tupelo?" Sam was already pouring his second cup of coffee.

"Mostly a two-bit thug. However, lately, he's been running with a much tougher crowd. He was found last night overturned in his car less than a mile from Julie Davenport's house. How's that for coincidence? At first glance, it appeared to be nothing more than a reckless driving accident, that is, until they pulled his body out."

"Yeah?"

"You know what he looked like, Sam?"

"Like a guy that got on the wrong side of a German Shepherd and a couple of angry house cats?"

Joe tried unsuccessfully not to grin. "Yeah. What I'd like to know is which one of those animals can shoot a Sig Sauer with crackerjack accuracy."

Sam whistled. "I'm pretty sure that requires opposable thumbs." He paused and shook his head. "Why is it that every time we get close, it turns out we're still flying at night by the seat of our pants?"

"Suppose you tell me what you were doing last night, besides getting Julie Davenport out of a speeding ticket?"

Sam recounted all that had happened since he first heard her license number broadcast over the scanner.

"You spent the night! Oh, Sam, of all the stupid…"

"In another bedroom, all right? I don't even know what she wore to bed, okay? C'mon, Joe. She was terrified and completely exhausted. Her house was in shambles. Somebody went into a rage filled rampage. No way could I leave her alone like that. It was nearly dawn and we were both spent."

"Okay, okay. I still don't like it. So Tupelo told her to give him the list? What did she say about that? How did she explain it?"

"She didn't. In the state she was in, I was not about to question her. I just asked her to tell me what happened. I'll get the details later today."

"Right. But there's still a problem with the timeline here. Tupelo attacked Julie at approximately 9:15 p.m., or possibly a little earlier. According to Julie's story, he ran out of the house and she, of course, wasted no time getting to the animal hospital with the dog. Her license number was reported at 9:35, which lines up okay. According to the coroner, Tupelo was shot between 9:20 and 9:30 p.m. Routine patrol car stopped within minutes of his death, so the kill was fresh. Julie had to have driven right past him, but we'll allow for her state of mind and speed of travel, and say she didn't notice him. His car was off the road, so he may not have even been visible to a speeding driver. Now, if her house was trashed by the time she arrived back home, when? About 3:00 a.m.? Who did it?"

"Whoever shot Manny Tupelo."

"The list was not in her house. It was not in the Jaguar. Too bad about Manny Tupelo, but he was expendable. He had been warned. What do we do about Ms. Davenport? We still do not know what she knows." The captain was angry. His brow was furrowed, his jaw set, as he clenched and unclenched his fist, staring at his top agent.

"I will find out what she knows and dispose of her. At this point, it would be my pleasure."

"Do you think she's dealing with somebody else? What happened to the money?"

"I think Jack absconded with the money, double-crossing everybody."

"It's possible. We know the money left Switzerland, but it's been impossible to clearly trace since then. The list never surfaced and the goods never arrived. What do you suspect she knows?"

"More than she's letting on. Nothing would satisfy me more than watching her face as her final betrayal sinks in."

The captain was not satisfied. "I believe you are right, that Jack stole the money and got clean away. At least until the plane crashed. Small consolation," he snorted. "Did the money also burn? I doubt it. However, there is no trace of the money, the package, or the list. It's somewhere. It's all somewhere." He was pacing as his frustration grew. He continued, "The only person who can answer all of these questions is dead, but I cannot believe his grieving widow knows nothing."

"I will find out for sure."

"Time is running out."

They discussed more plans and he waved his agent away.

Julie returned as the clean-up crew was preparing to leave. "Ms. Davenport, did you want us to dispose of your ripped up furniture and drapes for you? We have a truck, if you would like us to take them now."

Julie was pleasantly surprised at the efficiency of the crew. All the blood stains were gone. Everything had been thoroughly cleaned. The only things out of place were the pieces of furniture that had been destroyed. She told them to have at it and thanked them for their work.

She called the animal hospital and was informed that Fred was recovering nicely and could come home in about three days. Great. She missed him terribly.

She had no sooner replaced the receiver, when the phone rang. It was Sam.

"Feel like company for dinner?"

"Sure. But do you think he'll be back tonight? I mean, somebody has been here all day. I feel uneasy about leaving the house empty, especially without Fred here. Unless you want to go through it room by room again." *Or stay the night again, which would make me feel even better, but I'm not going to be the one to suggest it.*

"No problem. And no, I feel quite confident that your attacker will not be back. We'll talk over dinner. Pick you up in an hour."

"Where are we going?"

"Nosy, aren't you? Why do you need to know?"

"Because if we go out for burgers, I wear jeans and a t-shirt. If we go out for prime rib, I wear a dress. Are you sure you're a detective?"

"Go for the dress."

Sam wouldn't be there for an hour. Plenty of time to get ready. She needed to call Meg.

"Where've you been? You missed all the excitement. I'm getting new furniture, by the way."

"Out with boyfriend number eight hundred fifty-four. I've got stuff to tell you, too. How 'bout we order pizza at your house tonight, rent a movie, and pop popcorn with lots of butter?"

"I'd love to, but I can't tonight. Got plans."

"You? Plans? You can practice or wash your hair anytime, you know."

"If I was rich, I'd buy better friends."

"You are rich. Try again."

"I, um, I'm going out to dinner."

"With a *guy*? What, Julie, boyfriend number two?"

I'm beginning to wish. "No, no. We're just friends, that's all." *Plus, he thinks I murdered my husband, but I try not to let little details like that cloud my life.*

"You don't feel guilty going out so soon after Jack?"

Thanks, Meg. I needed that. See if I tell you he slept here last night. "We're just friends, Meg, nothing more. I gotta go. How about a rain check for tomorrow?"

"You're on. And I want details."

"There won't be any."

Julie showered quickly. She decided to put up her long, red curls. That done, she put on fresh make-up and perfume and chose a deep turquoise, form fitting, side-slit dress with a v-neck and multi-spaghetti straps that hugged a plunging, open back. She added gold dangly earrings, matching necklace and bracelet, and strappy turquoise spiked heels. She admired the effect in her mirror, noting how well she cleaned up. Especially after last night. The combination of turquoise and gold set off her auburn hair and electric blue eyes. She looked, in fact, stunning.

Sam was punctual, as she expected. She noted with a mixture of satisfaction and discomfort that he could not take his eyes off her when she opened the door.

"Julie Davenport, you take my breath away," he exclaimed.

She could feel herself blushing and tried to will the blush back by concentrating on something else, like trees or cement mixing. He looked nice as well, but she had never seen him wear anything but a suit, so she didn't have anything for comparison.

They arrived at an elegant, downtown restaurant and were ushered into a candle-lit, corner booth. Sam ordered for both of them. Julie didn't know if she was more excited to be with this kind, handsome gentleman or nervous because she was a suspect and he had a job to do. She thought ruefully, that if this is what her life had come down to, then she really needed to get out more often.

"How are you doing after your ordeal? I see you took the bandages off and covered the stitches in Band-Aids. They're barely visible. The cuts are already healing nicely. It doesn't look like you will have scars."

"It helps knowing Fred will be okay and also having so many people in the house. After a good night's rest and a shower, I feel better than I would have thought after last night. You said my attacker wouldn't be bothering me. Was he caught? Do I have to identify him in a line-up or something?"

"Julie, was this the man?" Sam showed her a photo of Manny Tupelo. Julie's face whitened and her hand shook as she studied the photograph. She nodded silently as she stared, unable to take her eyes off of the photo. She swallowed hard through clenched teeth.

"Is he in jail? Can he get out on bail?"

"He's in the morgue at the moment."

Julie nodded. She did not want to know the details, but she wasn't sorry to hear it.

"Julie, you told me last night that he demanded a list from you. What kind of list did he want?"

"I have no idea. Sam, this has not only been terribly frightening for me, but I don't know when I have ever been more confused. You seem to believe Jack was murdered, but I can't believe he could have had any enemies. He was a wonderful and generous man. Yet, I went out to the airfield where he kept his jet and the mechanic he trusted to maintain the plane is nowhere to be found. Even though he was fired, he hasn't even bothered to come in to pick up his final paycheck and it's been months! I had many questions I wanted to ask him. I've tried calling Jack's business number and it's been disconnected. I've been followed, harassed on the telephone, had my home broken into, and been attacked. My dog is in the hospital and my newest friend is a detective who wants answers from me. Well, I don't have any answers, but I have a whole pack of questions, so why don't we turn the tables and you start giving me some answers for a change?" Her voice gradually rose in pitch and volume as she talked.

"I see you're feeling better," he answered, shifting uneasily in his seat. "Julie, I'm sorry. I didn't mean to upset you. Have another glass of wine. Let's talk about something else."

"I don't *want* another glass of wine. I don't *want* to talk about something else. I want to know what's going on. I want to know what you suspect about my late husband."

"Julie, I could not give you that information if I wanted to."

"Is this supposed to be dinner or a romantic interrogation?"

"Dinner."

Is he lying?

"With a very beautiful lady."

Nice save. "Do you believe I murdered my husband, or conspired to murder my husband?"

"No, Julie, in all honesty, I do not. I am just trying to get some answers to a very puzzling case. Which, by the way, I wouldn't mind dropping for tonight, if you don't mind?"

Julie searched his deep brown eyes. She wanted to trust him. She needed him to trust her. It was bad enough to imagine Jack was murdered, but it was of paramount importance to her that Sam believed her incapable of that crime, whatever else he might have thought of her. "I could never trust you if I thought you believed I could have killed him."

"I don't, okay?"

This was not going well and Julie wished they could start this evening over. She was not going to get her answers and she could tell Sam wanted to get off the entire topic. She was uncomfortable and she could tell he was too. Their salads arrived, creating a much needed diversion. Good time to change the subject.

"Guess what I did today?" she asked brightly, entirely unaware that Sam already knew every move she had made, every person she talked to, and every route she had traveled.

"Tell me, what did you do today?" Sam asked, smiling sweetly at her.

Why is he smiling like that? What is he up to? She smoothed her napkin in her lap and straightened her posture.

"I replaced all the damaged furniture and carpeting that your clean-up crew carted out of my house. By the way, they were wonderful. And thanks for having my car delivered. I wish today's purchases were being delivered as quickly."

"My pleasure."

Dinner was served; grilled, wild salmon in a wine and dill sauce, fresh grilled asparagus wrapped in smoked bacon, sprinkled with parmesan cheese, and new potatoes with butter and parsley. Julie was hungrier than she realized. The salad had not abated her appetite. As she ate her dinner, she began to relax and once again felt comfortable talking to Sam.

She told him how she had rescued the cats when they were kittens from a shelter and how she was a strong believer in rescue animals. She pontificated on the evils of purchasing a pet when there were so many sweet, wonderful animals waiting to be adopted from the shelters, although she did admit that Jack had bought Fred. But Fred was specially trained and given the most recent events, it was a good thing.

"So do you have any pets?" she asked him.

"I like animals a lot, had dogs, cats, and a turtle growing up, but my schedule doesn't allow for a pet at this time. I'm away from home too much and it wouldn't be fair to a pet to be left alone for so many hours."

She nodded in agreement, pleased with Sam's answer.

Dessert arrived. Sam chose an apple tart, but knew Julie well enough by this time to order chocolate lava cake, which clearly delighted her. He watched in puzzled amazement as she relished it, closing her eyes with each bite and breathing deeply. *Is she actually moaning when she swallows?* He had never seen someone experience dessert quite like she was. Not wanting to be rude, he refused to laugh at her and tried hard not to stare. He resisted the temptation to ask her if she wanted to take her dessert someplace where she could be alone with it. Never before had he witnessed anyone devour a dessert in such a sensual manner.

Dessert was followed with coffee for Sam and hot cocoa with butterscotch schnapps for Julie.

"Have you heard anything from Su Li? How is her mother?" Sam was well aware that Julie had spoken with Su Li earlier. He hated that every question he asked her, he either already knew the answer to, or worse, sounded like she was being interrogated.

"She's worse. It's just a matter of time. Su Li says there is no hope. My heart breaks for her. This is a woman who has known nothing but sorrow and tragedy, yet still had so much love and compassion to give to others. She was full of wisdom and graciousness. In spite of all the hardship she has endured, she lived her life with dignity and strength. This seems so unfair." Julie told Sam about the boating accident and Miyso's kindness to her.

Sam listened intently as Julie shared her painful memory of her last summer at the lake. He longed to comfort her and realized he was struggling to remain objective about Julie.

"Surely you know by now, that your parents did not blame you for Philip's death. I trust that issue was resolved?"

"Yes. They were just overcome with deep grief. It was Daddy who felt guilty. He was afraid he had lost both of his children when he was swept away. They were torn between watching me lying unconscious in a hospital bed and burying Philip, so when Miyso offered to stay with me, they made their peace with a terrible situation and went home with Philip's body. As a young child, of course, I did not understand. I was almost ready to graduate high school when we finally were able to talk about it and they were mortified to learn I had blamed myself. They sold the cabin the month after Philip's funeral and we never returned to the area."

"Are your parents still living? Do they know what you have been going through?"

"No. Mother became very ill with an inoperable brain tumor only a few months after I moved back to St. Louis to play for the symphony. Daddy stayed by her side constantly. She had the best care possible, of course. By that time, Daddy was Chief of Surgery and the best of everything was at our disposal, but nothing could be done. She died peacefully with both of us beside her. It tore my heart. But she did not suffer long and for that we were grateful."

"I'm sorry, Julie."

"Several months later, I had my first big solo. I got Daddy and Su Li great seats so they could hear me. But afterwards, when the house lights came up, I looked for him and his seat was empty. I knew right away something was terribly wrong. Daddy would have never missed my solo. Su Li and I drove to his house and as we arrived, an ambulance was just leaving. He'd had a heart attack and did not make it through the night. It was very difficult for him without Mom there. I don't think he wanted to go on without her. He missed her. I miss them both." She looked away from Sam.

They left the restaurant subdued and drove back to Pineview in comfortable silence, both of them aware that their unlikely friendship had attained a higher level.

As he promised, Sam went through the entire house, room by room, checking windows, doors, closets, and anything else that might prove to be a hiding place. All he found were the cats. He did not dare to tell Julie that whoever killed Manny Tupelo might have Julie in mind as his next victim. He hoped he would be able to protect her.

He found her downstairs in the cozy hearth room, since the living room had no furniture in it. "I pronounce you safe and sound. When does your new furniture arrive?"

"Some of it next week, some not until three more weeks, can you believe it? I have to sleep in one of the guest rooms again."

"I guess I ought to be going now." He paused, hoping she would object. "It's getting late." *I wish you would ask me to stay. I am afraid for you and I can't tell you why. I can't tell you anything. Please ask me to stay. Just say the word and I will stay.*

She walked him to the door, hesitatingly. He held her hands in his and pulled her to him. He kissed her tenderly, touched her cheek, ready to remain with her if she would only ask.

But she did not.

She watched him get into his car and drive off. *I wish you would have stayed with me. I feel so much safer when you are with me. Why couldn't you be a better mind reader?* Then she locked and bolted the door. It seemed like she was being held captive in her own home and although she lived in luxuriant spaciousness, she felt claustrophobic. *I'm locked in. Everybody else is locked out. I don't even have Fred.*

Last time, though, Meg had checked everything, and somebody got in anyway. Julie decided to start on the top floor and work her way down until she was sure herself, that the house was secure. It took her more than an hour. By the time she finished, she was bone-tired. Every time the floor creaked, she stiffened with fear. The slightest noise made her jump. She kept expecting someone to lunge at her with a knife. But eventually, she became convinced that she was, indeed, alone in the house. With her bed gone, Johann and Sebastienne followed Julie through the house until she picked out her room and turned down the bed. They leapt onto the bed, purring, inviting her to join them.

14

The sun streamed softly through the guest room, sparkling like tiny diamonds through the white sheers that covered the windows, bathing Julie in gentle light. She awoke placidly, basking in the warmth of the sunshine, like the lazy felines who slept peacefully in bed with her. She opened her eyes to see the light bouncing off the wall, appreciative of the soothing warmth permeating the soft, comfortable bedding. She looked around, not knowing where she had awakened at first.

Oh, yeah. One of the guest rooms.

It was decorated, as were all the rooms, by Jack or whomever Jack had hired to do the decorating. The room was painted white with bright green stripes and accented in yellow. The bedspread was white with yellow flowers and butterflies and the curtains were bright green, held back by butterfly tiebacks. White sheers hung between the curtains, allowing shimmery sunlight to filter in. It was a friendly looking room and Julie guessed the color scheme had been picked because the windows faced east to pick up the brightness of the morning sun. If the intent was to put a morning riser in a cheerful mood, it was working.

Julie showered, dressed, applied fresh bandages, and started downstairs for breakfast. She noticed her answering machine flashing and remembered she had not checked it last night.

At least it isn't Manny Tupelo. She pushed the button with confidence.

"Hi, Julie, this is Stanley Goldman. Sheila and I wanted to make sure everything was all right with you. We heard you were taking a leave after your house was broken into. We are worried about you, dear. Should we be? Please call us soon." Julie grinned. *If they're worrying about me, at least they're happy.* Neither Stanley, nor Sheila could be happy without something to worry about. *It's nice to know the gossip lines are open and working at The Hall.* Julie had been so upset when she called Terry, she had temporarily forgotten that everything was public knowledge ten minutes after someone knew anything that could be considered remotely juicy. She would call the Goldmans later to put them at ease. She knew how much they enjoyed worrying about her.

There was a knock at the back door and Julie was glad to see Meg.

"Hey there!"

"Hey there, yourself. It's gorgeous outside. Want to go for a walk?" Meg was wearing jeans, a t-shirt and a lightweight jacket. She called for Fred, but of course, he didn't come running. "What gives, Julie? Where's your baby?"

"He's recovering at the hospital after being stabbed by the head case you told me got his jollies from being obnoxious over the telephone."

"What has been going on around here, anyway? Enough to deplete your supply of orgasmic chocolate? Come on. Let's go for a walk. It's a glorious day. Fabulous weather. Nothing like fresh air."

They left through the back door, Julie locking it securely behind her, and walked slowly through the woods. She was grateful for Meg's company. As they walked together, she told her friend all that had happened since they had last spoken. They came to a wide clearing in the middle of the woods and Meg stopped and turned to face Julie.

"So did he kiss you last night?"

"Meg! I was nearly killed! My house was torn apart and my dog is in the hospital and all you want to know is if he kissed me? Helloooo, Meg!"

"Well, did he?"

Julie rolled her eyes. "If you must know, yes."

"Did you kiss him back?"

"Meg, what is the matter with you?"

"Did you?"

"Yes. Satisfied?"

"I thought you loved Jack."

"I did love Jack. I loved him very deeply."

"So less than nine months after his death, you're kissing another man?"

"It doesn't mean I didn't love Jack. Meg, Jack is gone. I'll never stop loving him. For a long time, it seemed as if my life was over. I didn't plan this. And I certainly wasn't looking for it. Besides, the circumstances are so weird. It just happened. It was just a kiss. I never claimed to be in love with Sam. I will always love Jack."

"You're not the only one, princess."

"What?"

"You are so stupid." Meg's country twang was gone, replaced by a harsh tone Julie did not recognize. "Jack and I were in love. I loved him more than you ever could have."

"Meg! What are you talking about?" Julie felt her mouth go dry as she took a step backward. Her stomach twisted into knots, as if she had been kicked.

"*I* was supposed to marry him. *I* knew him first. *I* loved him first and *he loved me*." She was hissing now, spewing anger and jealousy with the vehemence of a red, hot volcano. Her words hit Julie hard. "We were in this together. But he needed you, so he set up Davenport Enterprises. You were his cover and it worked for a while."

"I…I don't understand."

Meg half snorted, half laughed. "Jack was smuggling arms, Julie. He used you to get the list of buyers and suppliers to

Europe. He never told me how. We used to laugh at you when you would say your husband was in the import-export business. You had no idea. Oh, he was importing and exporting, all right!"

Julie felt as if the earth was tilting. *How could this be true? That's the list that Manny Tupelo wanted and he was willing to kill for it.*

"It was Jack's idea for us to become friends. It was his idea for me to befriend the woman he was sleeping with when *I* was the one he loved. *I* was the one who loved *him*. And now, you are already with another man, as if Jack meant nothing to you."

"No, Meg." Julie could not believe what she was hearing.

"I even picked out your dog. Fred, and that's a stupid name for such a magnificent animal by the way, but he knew me before he knew you. That's why it was so easy for me to get into your house. It's also the reason I drugged him instead of killing him. You were so gullible."

Julie was reeling. *How can this be?* "No. You … you're wrong. You were my friend. I trusted you. We were friends. I loved Jack and *he loved me*."

"*I* loved Jack and he *used* you. The whole time he was with me. You meant nothing to him, you and your perfect little life. So, what does it feel like to be betrayed, cupcake?" She reached into the pocket of her jacket and pulled out a pistol. Julie backed away from her, fighting rising panic and shaking with revulsion at Meg's shocking disclosure.

Meg raised the pistol, aiming straight at Julie. "Betrayed by your husband who had me first? Betrayed by your best friend? I was the one who left the window unlocked the other night. I needed to get in and find the list Jack hid. He never would tell his secret. I figured it was in his precious car when I couldn't find it in your house. I was the one who slashed your stuff when Manny stabbed your dog. Of course, I knew him. The only reason you have been allowed to live is because we didn't know what you knew. Only now, I know that you know nothing. Nothing except what I've told you, and I can't possibly let you live knowing that, can I?"

She stepped toward Julie, steadily pointing the gun, as Julie, staring wide-eyed, backed away from her.

"The last thought you will carry to your grave is that the only people you trusted betrayed you. Small satisfaction for me, but I'll take what I can get. Say goodbye, Julie," she spat.

Meg raised the gun, taking careful aim. Julie screamed as the sound of a report echoed through the wooded hills. But it was Meg who dropped to the ground, a bullet shot through her head, her own gun unfired lay beside her, and her wide, sightless eyes bearing a final expression of hateful disbelief. Julie looked around frozen in terror, but saw no one. The woods, with their heavy foliage could have hidden an army, so a lone gunman would have all the protection he needed. She could not even tell from which direction the shot had been fired. All she knew was she had to get out of there.

She ran, stumbling back to the house, looking back over her shoulder, but seeing no one. She finally reached home, gasping, and with trembling hands, fumbled to unlock her door, dropping her keys twice. Once inside her house, she locked and bolted the door behind her.

Sam, Sam, I have to call Sam...have to reach Sam. Where is his card? He had given her at least two. Why couldn't she find one? *It's here some place. Had it been thrown out by the cleaning crew?* She couldn't find it anywhere. She ran to several of the windows and looked outside, searching the woods frantically for any sign of the gunman, but the woods were deceptively still. *What if he's in the house?* She could not find Sam's card.

Okay, okay, Julie, just calm down. Think! I'll just call the Pineview Police and ask for him. They can put me in touch with him. Okay, fine, no reason to panic. He can be here within minutes. She found the number in the phone book and dialed it.

"Pineview Police Department. How may I help you?"

"Uh, hello. May I speak with Detective Sam Hernandez, please?"

"Who did you say?"

"Sam Hernandez. He's a detective, and I've lost his card. I need to reach him. *Please!*"

"No, ma'am. I'm sorry, there's no Hernandez here at Pineview."

"But he's been working on my case. This is Julie Davenport. He's been handling—"

"Ms. Davenport, we have no one here by that name. And the only time your name comes up on my computer is when we notified you of your husband's death back in January. And yes, I see you reported a break-in several days ago. But there has never been a Sam Hernandez here and we are not aware of any active case involving you. I'm sorry."

Julie's blood ran cold. She shook, overwhelmed with fear and doubt. *Who is he?* Was she so stupid she had fallen for two men who were dangerous criminals? Was she that bad a judge of character?

I gotta get out of here. I gotta get out of here now. She ran to her closet, pulled out a few changes of clothing, hurriedly packed and threw the suitcase in the trunk of the Maxima. She rushed down to the basement and picked up the cat carriers. *This* would be loads of fun. Johann and Sebastienne were still sleeping in the sunbeam peacefully warming the bed she slept in last night. She unceremoniously shoved them into their respective carriers, locking them in. They were placed onto the floorboard in the back seat, yowling and carrying on at the indignities they were rudely forced to suffer. She carried out her cello and strapped it into the front seat. Ten minutes had already passed. Couldn't waste any more time. The shooter could be anywhere. It was probably Sam. He had a way of showing up far too often and conveniently. Why had she not seen that? How could she have trusted him? She had to leave. She ran back into the hearth room for her chocolates. Seeing Jack's chair, she tasted bile in her throat. She violently removed her wedding rings, and hurled them to the floor. Turning to her answering machine, she erased the entire memory, grabbed her purse and ran to the car. She backed out of the garage, looking frantically about and seeing no one, took off, the cats still making a ruckus in the back seat. *I can't leave Fred. Sam will know to wait for me at Dr. Medcalf's.*

She drove to the animal hospital, circling the block with the stealth of a tiger stalking prey, watching for suspicious cars, and seeing nothing unusual, parked in back of the building. She entered through the employees' door. Pam Medcalf looked up from a chart she was reading. She raised her eyebrows in surprise at Julie's unusual entrance.

"Julie, we were not expecting you until tomorrow."

"I know. Is there any way I can pick up Fred now? Is he well enough to leave?"

"He could, but he needs to be kept quiet for a few days. No running through the woods or up and down the stairs at home. Can you see to that?"

"No problem. I just really want to take him now."

"All right. I'll have an assistant bring him out to the car. Let me give you his antibiotics and sedatives. One pill twice a day until they're gone for the antibiotics, one sedative if he gets active. He needs to stay quiet. Any oozing or other problems, bring him right back. Otherwise, we don't need to see him for ten more days to remove the stitches. He's still partially sedated, so he'll be groggy for a few more hours. Questions?"

"No, that's fine. Back seat, please." Julie paid the bill while Fred, ecstatic to see her in spite of his drug-induced grogginess, was helped to the car. She rushed out to see him. "How's Mama's baby, huh? Calm down, big boy, take it easy." Now she had everybody in her little car. *Now, where?* She thought about leaving Missouri, but what if the roads were blocked? What if they were looking for her along the interstates? Those would be the most popular routes. She left Pineview and drove around on the side roads for several minutes, thinking. Where could she go where she and her pets would be safe and welcome? Where could she go where nobody would think to look for her? Stanley and Sheila Goldman's. They were the only people she could think of. The pets would be a terrible imposition, but she had no choice. She needed a place to stay and the Goldmans could be trusted. She would do everything she could to repay them.

She kept an SLSO directory in her glove compartment. Pulling into a Steak 'n' Shake parking lot, she looked up their address. Bingo. University City. *About as far on the other side of the St. Louis metropolitan area as you can get from Pineview.* Julie drove only the back roads, staying off the highways, constantly searching her rearview mirror, confident she was not being followed. It took her more than an hour to reach the Goldman's neighborhood. She crept along the quiet, tree-lined street until she found their address. Their driveway wound all the way to the back of the house. So far, so good. Her car would not be visible from the street. Julie parked in back, cracked the car windows and walked quickly up the path to the Goldman's back door.

Stanley and Sheila were sitting on the back porch eating a late lunch. Julie remembered how they had treated her with exceptional kindness after Jack's death. She was fond of both of them. They were childless and Julie was without parents, so in their own way, they filled a need in each other. She hoped her request would not test the limits of their friendship.

They looked delighted and surprised to see Julie approaching. They rose to greet her, but soon their expressions sobered.

"Julie, dear, you're deathly white and shaking so! What's wrong, child? Please, sit down. Here, some tea. Oh, Stanley, do you see her hands shaking? Julie, my dear, your hands are shaking. Do you see this, Stanley?"

"Yeah, Sheila, of course I see it, whaddaya think, I'm blind? Julie, you're shaking like a leaf. Whatsa matter, doll?"

Julie's attempt to remain calm and explain her predicament was in vain. As soon as she started to speak, she began to cry uncontrollably, overwhelmed by her final scene with Meg, and the realization that she had trusted Sam, even fallen for him, and he, too, was after her—whoever he was. Her shoulders shook as tears poured from her eyes, turning her face red.

"Oh no," Sheila exclaimed. "She's overcome. Poor dear. Stanley, do you see this? She's overcome. Here, Julie. I'll fix you some soup. Would you like some soup, dear?"

"Sheila, it's the middle of August. Nobody in their right mind wants soup in the middle of August. She wants a sandwich. Fix the child a sandwich."

"No, thank you, I'm not really hungry." Listening to the Goldmans' banter, which Julie always found humorous, made it easier for her to regain her composure. She sniffed one final time, and began, "I need to talk to you."

"She needs to talk. Stanley, let the girl talk. Talk to us, Julie. You know you can tell us anything. We heard about your break-in. How terrible for you! It goes on all over, it's just terrible. Talk to us, sweetie."

"Sheila, she can't talk with your mouth running, all right? Be quiet and let her speak. What's the trouble, Julie?"

"I need a place to stay for a few days," she began.

"Well, of course, you'll stay with us, no need to ask. We'd be delighted, wouldn't we, Stanley?"

"Certainly, dear. You are always welcome here, you know that."

"There's a slight problem. I have my cats and my German Shepherd. They're all well behaved. The only trouble is they shed so much, but I have no place else to go with them, and my shepherd was injured by the intruder and needs me to care for him. I know it's a terrible imposition, but—"

"Nonsense." Stanley cut her off mid-sentence. "Julie, you're in some sort of danger, aren't you? Bring your animals in. It's fine, don't worry. Hair, schmair. So we'll vacuum."

"Really? Oh, thank you! Thank you so much!" She hugged them both, then pulled away, holding them at arms' length. "Stanley, Sheila, I have to ask you one more thing. You know how at The Hall, anybody's business is everybody's business? Please, please, *please* keep this confidential. *Nobody* can know we are here. You must not let *anybody* know where I am."

Stanley shot Sheila a warning look. "She means nobody, Sheila. Keep quiet."

Sheila rolled her eyes at her husband with an exasperated look in response, then turned her back on him and said to Julie in a comforting voice, "Don't worry dear. You and your dog and your cats are all safe here. Nobody's sayin' nuthin' to nobody."

They settled her in the guest room. Stanley volunteered to go to the store for pet supplies. In her haste, Julie had forgotten food, litter, and litter boxes.

Sheila wanted to talk to Julie. They had not seen her lately and she knew something big, something important, even dangerous was going on. But Julie looked so weary and haggard; she wanted her to get some rest, so she turned back Julie's bed and ordered her into it. Her furry menagerie followed as if on cue.

Fifteen minutes later, Sheila checked on a sleeping Julie. The bed appeared to be covered with stuffed animals surrounding the pretty girl who slept so peacefully, only these animals were breathing. Looking at the cuddled up balls around Julie, Sheila indulged her brief fantasy of being a mother to a little girl with long, red curls. It passed, as had all her fantasies of motherhood years ago. It was not in God's plan to bless her and Stanley with children. She closed the door softly, turning the handle to avoid the click, and went into the kitchen to make sure Julie would not starve when she awoke. Soup would be a good start, even in August.

"She lost your card identifying you as a member of Pineview's finest."

"What are you talking about?"

Joe played the recording of Julie's conversation that morning. They could hear the breathless panic in her voice. But even before the dispatcher told her that Sam was not who he had carefully been posing as, she sounded terrified. "We have to get out there, Joe."

"Let's go."

The grey sedan pulled up under the canopy in front of The Monstrosity, and the two men got out. They circled the house, trying the doors and found everything locked. Sam looked through the window of the garage and with a sinking feeling in his gut noted Julie's car was gone. "We need to get into the house."

"Why, Sam? She's gone."

"I need to see if the cats are there. If she left her pets, she'll be back."

They broke in through the garage window and entered the lifeless house. Sam called the cats by name and searched their favorite haunts for them. No luck. Finally, he went to the kitchen and pressed the electric can opener. When the sound of the can opener elicited no response, he slammed his fist on the counter. They looked around the house, searching for any kind of clue but found none. In the hearth room, Sam stepped on something hard. He bent down and picked up Julie's wedding rings, holding them up for Joe to see. They exchanged worried looks. He pressed the button on her phone to check for messages. "She erased everything on her answering machine. Her cello's gone, too. What happened here?"

Joe asked, "You said she has no cell phone, right? What's with that? Can't be the money. They're becoming all the rage. I would have thought she'd have one."

"Yeah. She's got her own views about cell phones. She has one of those old car phones, but I have no information about it. Nobody uses those things anymore."

They walked around the grounds and noticed turkey vultures, which were plentiful in Pineview, circling further out on the Davenport property. Might as well check it out. They found Meg's body, a single shot through the head. "Same Sig Sauer that killed Manny Tupelo, I'd bet the rent. She's not here, Sam. Let's go."

"She could have been taken. What if they took her?"

"All right. Before we get our exercise jumping to conclusions, let's see if we can locate the dog. If she took her dog, we at least have a timeline to start with. I'll have Keisha call the locals and report the body— as long as they know this is our jurisdiction."

They checked the animal hospital and to no one's surprise, learned Julie had taken Fred nearly three hours ago.

"Three hours. She could be close to the Arkansas border, in Springfield, halfway to Chicago, Paducah, Memphis, anywhere. She could be *anywhere*." Sam threw his pen down in disgust.

"I don't suppose you thought to plant a tracker in her car when you had the opportunity?"

Sam's shoulders drooped under the weight of defeat. "No. I was so concerned about the attack and keeping her safe, I didn't think to do so. She was being watched so closely, I didn't think it was necessary." Joe let it go.

"You seem to know her pretty well. Would she have boarded her pets and taken a plane?"

"No way. She would never leave Fred in his condition. Her pets are her children. She's either traveling, or she's hiding some place, but whichever, we need to be looking for a woman with two cats and an injured German Shepherd."

Joe wasted no time calling in an APB with Julie's name and a description of her and her zoo.

"At least there can't be too many people out there fitting that description. We'll find her."

They returned to their rented office space filled with maps, electronic equipment and portable file cabinets. Keisha had nothing to report. No news was not good news.

"The vet knew nothing except that Julie was in a hurry. Her friend and nearest neighbor, Meg is dead. Somehow, she's tied up in this. There has been no contact today with Su Li." Sam continued, "I guess we should start with the symphony members. From what Julie told me, there are no secrets in that group. Somebody will know something and as I understand it, musicians like to talk."

"I'll send Keisha. She's friendly, has a beautiful smile and is more likely to dig up something than either of us."

The captain sat at his desk thinking and stroking his mustache. He still believed Julie Davenport held the key. He was not happy. Meg Curtis was his top agent, but her personal vendetta against Julie had clouded her professional judgment and risked the entire operation. It was unfortunate she needed to be eliminated, but she had lost her perspective, causing her status to fall from that of a valuable asset to a dangerous liability. He frowned, thinking of the waste. Meg had endured living in a trailer, assuming a character vastly different from her own to build a credible cover. She had sacrificed much for the organization, but her secret hatred for the Davenport woman consumed her and in the end, sealed her fate.

The captain sighed heavily. It was true, he supposed, that if you wanted a job done right, you had to do it yourself. Although, he admitted to himself, the arms business in South America, Asia and the Middle East was profitable enough. Jack Davenport had been the best agent between Europe and the United States, and he managed to skip with both the money and the list of suppliers and buyers. He had all the plans and routes for everything. If the ATF got their hands on that list...

Jack had been entrusted with too much. He was smart and daring. Now, he was dead and the captain assumed the money had burned with the plane, unless it was sitting somewhere in a bank account in Switzerland, the Cayman Islands, or who knew where. The money trail was lost.

Julie was Jack's key to Europe, but how? If she had information, or was, in fact, involved, he had to find out what it was before he killed her. But, if she was, indeed, innocent, what purpose would be served in disposing of a woman who posed no threat to him? He actually disliked killing, found it rather distasteful, but it was a necessary evil required to protect his interests. Did that make him a bad person?

Sam was deflated. He had left Julie his card at least three different times. How could she have lost all of them? Professionally, this was only a setback. They would find her. What was most defeating was that after bending over backwards to earn her trust, he had now lost that trust and Julie with it. Did they have her now? Did they catch her after she retrieved Fred from the animal hospital? She was in certain danger, no matter where she was. Who killed Meg, and why? What had happened in Julie's woods? What did she know? If he had been truthful with her from the beginning, she would be safe with him now. He didn't care if she never forgave him. He didn't care if she never wanted to see him for the rest of her life. He wouldn't blame her. He just wanted to know she was safe. He put his head in his hands and rubbed his temples.

"Sam, we have other angles to work on this." Joe interrupted his train of thought. "Come on, Sam. The two oldest rules in the book. Rule Number One, don't fall in love with a suspect. Rule Number Two, don't break Rule Number One."

"She's no longer a suspect. She's been a victim all along. Unless we find her, she'll die as somebody else's victim. So what other angles do you want to look at?"

"While you were playing hero to the damsel in distress, I asked the lab to go over the DNA from the crash site again. Something isn't right there. Nobody, and I mean nobody can find Russ Richards, Davenport's mechanic. I'm working on a different theory, but I need to get the lab results before we go chasing down rabbit holes. We should have their report soon."

Keisha Livingston knocked lightly on the door and entered from the adjoining make-shift office. She did most of the grunt work as part of her training; the thankless, boring tasks that seldom yielded results, but occasionally hit pay dirt and had to be done as a matter of procedure. "I've been listening to all of these tapes again and reviewing the transcripts I typed. Julie has an appointment with a man named Arturo, to have her bow hair replaced. Next Friday at three o'clock. Man, do you know that neighborhood? I wouldn't go there in broad daylight surrounded by armed bodyguards!"

"What makes you think a woman who is running for her life would keep an appointment to have her bow re-haired?"

Keisha smiled and disregarded the sarcasm, pleased that her boss showed interest in her opinion. "For one thing, she doesn't know that anyone else knows about the appointment, so she would feel safe keeping it. For another, she's a musician. Her instrument is her livelihood. I got a cousin who plays in the Chicago Philharmonic. He is meticulous about caring for his viola. Why would she be any different?

"Anyway, a little background on this Arturo guy, not that you asked. His name is Arturo Benedetto. Came over on the boat as a teenager. He's ancient now. He's been in business in the same location since that neighborhood was respectable and refuses to move, only put up bars and bullet-proof glass. Lives in a tiny apartment in the back of his shop. Rarely leaves. Does excellent work, but almost nobody goes to see him anymore because of the neighborhood. Julie has known him since she was twelve. I would assume she really likes and trusts him. Her bow probably gets worked on three or four times a year, the cello, I would think, at least twice a year. I called my cousin and asked." She beamed, proud of herself.

"I don't know, Keisha," Joe said. "I think it's a long shot."

"I'm inclined to go with Keisha on this," Sam offered. "It not only makes sense, it's the only thing we have to go on right now."

Joe replied, "You're assuming she stayed in town and didn't leave the state."

Sam answered, "I'm not assuming anything of the sort. But it's the only lead we have. Keisha is heading out to Powell Hall tomorrow to talk to Julie's co-workers. If any of them knows where she is, or even might be, we may have another lead. But until then, this is all we've got, and I say we go for it. We got nothin' else to go on. The worse that can happen is we're wrong…again."

Julie needed to call Su Li. She knew Su Li would be calling home soon, and no one would answer. Julie wasn't sure if she could ever return to her home. She called Wanh's house, hoping Su Li would be at the hospital, so she wouldn't have to talk to her. She breathed a sigh of relief when the answering machine came on. It was much easier to lie to an inanimate object than to a friend.

"Hi, Su Li. I wanted to see how Miyso and Wanh were, and you, of course. Just wanted you to know we had a terrible storm and it knocked out the power and there's just a lot of damage. I'm staying at a hotel until the power is restored and the roads are cleared, so I didn't want you to worry when you couldn't reach me. I miss you and am keeping you and your family in my prayers." She did not like lying, but she had to provide some plausible explanation when Su Li called and nobody answered the phone. Her friend had enough on her plate.

15

"Hot off the presses!" Keisha was waiving papers at Joe and Sam, still warm after being snatched from the fax machine.

Joe took them from her and read them to himself. "It's beginning to look like my hunch is panning out."

"Let's hear it."

Sam and Keisha pulled their chairs in a circle around Joe as he continued.

"This is from the lab. We know the plane caught fire and exploded on impact. There was one badly burned body in the wreckage. Search and Rescue found a torn piece of material that looked like part of a shirt, snagged on a rock a few yards from the crash site. When Jack Davenport's DNA was found on that scrap of material, which was later identified as matching the shirt he was wearing, we made a positive ID. And since he was the only one on the plane, we had no reason to look for anyone else. At that time, the accident did not appear suspicious. It was designed to look exactly as it appeared. Like an unfortunate accident."

"But when the money disappeared, the supplies were not delivered, the list was nowhere to be found, and circumstances began to not add up, we had to go back and look again at the accident," Sam added.

"Because given that set of circumstances it then looked like Davenport was murdered, either for what he had, or for what he knew, right?" Keisha asked.

Joe nodded and continued. "Right on all counts. But our investigation got us nowhere, and now, Julie Davenport is missing and presumably in a lot of danger. So, I got to thinking." He paused and gulped his coffee.

"And?" Sam and Keisha asked in unison.

"And I think we've been working this case from the wrong angle all along. So, I asked the lab to run the DNA from not only that scrap of shirt, but also from the burned body and any pieces of the plane that were recovered. I asked the lab to run a number of tests and to report every finding immediately." He held the papers up. "They found a second set of DNA which they are now attempting to identify. I believe it will be that of Russ Richards. The lab also found traces of an accelerant, which caused the fire to burn faster and hotter, ensuring nothing usable would be discovered in the event anyone got suspicious of the accident and launched a full scale investigation."

"How could one piece of shirt have DNA from two individuals?" Keisha asked.

Sam stared at Joe as the implication of Joe's hunch sunk in, and answered Keisha. "Because Jack Davenport planned *all* of this. Keisha, everyone that knew Davenport described him as friendly, outgoing, generous, romantic. Sheesh, the guy was nearly perfect. We know better. He was meticulous, ruthless, and cunning. Above all, he was an extremely dangerous criminal."

Keisha interrupted. "How could Julie fall in love with a guy like that? She isn't stupid."

"I have given that same question much thought," Sam answered. "And no, she isn't stupid at all, but she also doesn't have any street smarts. I think that, in fact, Julie was not really in love with Jack Davenport nearly as much as Julie was in love with being in love. Keisha, love isn't something you fall into like a hole in the ground. Love is something you grow into. Julie never had a real boyfriend. Despite her stage presence, which exudes grace, style, and confidence, she actually is rather awkward socially.

"A handsome, suave, slightly older man comes into her life, sweeps her off her feet, lavishes her with expensive gifts, they have a whirlwind romance and marriage. Her parents were deceased, so they couldn't advise her. Her only friend was Su Li. She had no one to bounce things off of besides Su Li, who is six years younger than Julie and no more experienced. I may be no expert on women, but I do know they always talk, especially about men. Julie didn't have any friends to talk to about Davenport, so no red flags were raised. She was the perfect patsy. She wouldn't know enough to question him. She was the ideal wife to provide him with a respectable cover.

"And he did whatever was necessary to keep her happy and in the dark as to his real reason for the quick romance and marriage. He was charming and used all that charm and personality not just to win her, but to manipulate her. She never had a clue. And that house? I checked the Recorder's office. That place was built long before they were married, but he had her convinced it was her wedding gift. He provided her everything she could possibly want, so it was easy to sweep her off her feet. What we still don't know is how he was getting information into and out of Europe. We believe she had something to do with it. But, I just don't think she was aware of it. After questioning her, I thought he had to be using her instrument, but she was flagged by customs on at least one occasion and nothing out of the ordinary was ever found."

"So why blow up the plane? Didn't he still need her?"

Joe answered. "Sam is right. Jack carefully planned all of this, right down to the last minute detail. What I think, is that he bought Russ Richards a bottle of his favorite beverage. Maybe he laced it, we'll probably never know, but that's a good bet, because he would need Richards to be unconscious. Anyway, he was able to get Richards on that plane and at some point before they were over the Rockies, I think he killed Richards, traded shirts with him to make sure his own DNA would be found, and before parachuting out of the plane with a boatload of money, doused Richards and the plane with the accelerant to be sure Richards would be so badly burned that he would be identified as Jack Davenport.

"I think he parachuted out with the arms payment as the plane flew nearer to the mountainside, and stayed around just long enough to watch the plane crash and burn. Then I think he planted the torn shirt piece after rubbing it over himself so his DNA would be found. Nobody was gonna miss Russ Richards. They would figure he was out on an alcoholic binge, and then after Davenport's plane went down he would be blamed for it, so it would look even more likely that he took off for parts unknown, when in truth, he was dead in Colorado."

"So if Jack Davenport faked his own death by putting Russ Richards' body in his place, then Jack could be coming back. Is Julie in danger?"

"Julie is in danger, all right," Sam answered, "but I don't think from Jack. He took the client's money, did not deliver the arms shipment to the client, double-crossed his organization, and convinced everyone he was dead. Which is what he will be if either the client or his organization finds him. *We* suspected Julie from the start. Wives usually know anywhere from something to everything. We know better now, but there are a lot of very bad people who still think she is involved. That's why I am worried about her. Davenport is in the wind. Probably relaxing on a beach somewhere with a nice cold drink, if he's smart, which he is.

"Were you able to interview the other symphony members, Keisha? Anything to report? Does anybody have any idea where she might be?"

"Sorry, Sam. I talked with most of the string players and other musicians who were about her age. Nobody knew anything. Nobody had any ideas. It was a dead end."

"We have to find her."

"I'm tellin' you, Sam. She will show up at Arturo's on Friday to have her bow re-haired. Even if you don't believe that, like you said yesterday, it's the only lead we have."

"Be careful, dear, please be careful. Stanley, tell Julie to be careful."

"Julie, Sheila's right. That neighborhood is terrible. Nobody goes to Arturo anymore. He should have moved west like everybody else." Stanley knew his words would fall on deaf ears.

"Stanley, Sheila, I appreciate your concern. But I've known Arturo since I was twelve. He's the best there is. I always go in daylight, and I'm always very careful. As long as Arturo's around, I could never go anywhere else. Anyway, after all I've been through, Arturo's neighborhood should be a cakewalk. Besides, I have this great new bow that Jack gave me. I've never used anything like it, and I really want to show it to Arturo. I'm quite anxious to get his opinion."

The Goldmans were unmoved. Their faces reflected worry and doubt over Julie leaving the safety of their comfortable home. They loved her and thought of her as the daughter they never had.

"Julie, honey, I forgot to tell you. Someone came around The Hall yesterday during rehearsal looking for you. A black lady in her twenties. She asked a lot of questions. Asked nearly all the string players if anyone had heard from you or knew how to get in touch with you. I am terribly worried." Sheila, like Julie, was a terrible liar, and Julie was concerned that Sheila had given up her whereabouts. Julie's heart began to race, fearing Sheila had somehow given something away. It was impossible for Sheila to keep a secret. Julie had no idea who the woman could have been, and began to wonder exactly how many people were after her and if she would ever be safe again.

Stanley spoke up before Julie had time to panic at Sheila's revelation. "Don't worry, doll. Sheila kept her big yap shut, I can promise you that. Nuthin' we said gave nuthin' away. You got my word on it. But we both agree you shouldn't see Arturo. At least not now, for heaven's sake."

"Look, I'll come straight home. Won't pass go, won't collect two hundred dollars, okay? I'll be fine." She hugged them, and before they could offer further objections, Julie was in her car, backing out of the driveway. She didn't want to be late, or Arturo would worry about her as well. Getting her bow re-haired in a neighborhood that looked like a war zone should be the easiest thing she had to do all week. Nonetheless, Julie was extremely cautious when driving, constantly checking to see if anyone was following her.

The captain waited patiently for Julie to arrive. Not normally a gambling man, he was betting Julie would keep her appointment. He stroked his mustache as he waited. His patience was beginning to wear thin. First, Manny Tupelo, with his sophomoric interference tipped her off, and then Meg screwed up. Wherever Julie had been staying, he believed she would come alone. Someone would have to be six kinds of crazy to voluntarily go to this part of town, for any reason. He checked his Sig Sauer, the silencer firmly locked in place, just in case he needed it. He would grab her and use whatever means necessary to obtain the information.

Julie cruised slowly past Arturo's little shop. She circled the block three times, searching for suspicious looking vehicles or people. There were a couple of pimp cars, another couple of stripped down cars, no doubt stolen and abandoned, and a van from the electric company parked on the block; about par for the course. The area looked the same as always. Boarded up buildings and mom-and-pop storefronts long out of business lined the street. Trash was strewn everywhere. Sounds of angry voices arguing about everything and nothing, wafted from somewhere not too far off. Welcome to Arturo's.

Julie, certain she had not been followed, parked directly in front of Arturo's place, several yards behind the utility van. Tightly clutching her prized bow, securely packed in its pouch, she hurried over shards of broken glass that littered the sidewalk, down the cracked and crumbling concrete steps to the door of the shop.

"Julie, my child, how are you?" The voice of sanity in the midst of craziness. Arturo sounded genuinely glad to see her. He had so few customers these days. The elderly gentleman, now stooped, hobbled over to the counter to greet his biggest fan. He wore a cheery smile, full of yellowed teeth. His pale blue eyes were rheumy as he studied Julie. "You've gotten so thin, my dear. I hope you've not been unwell." Arturo still had somewhat of a mane of white hair that looked as though he combed it with an electric toothbrush, but with his advancing years, it had thinned considerably, and now protruded erratically from his head like tufts of white cotton. Although nearly crippled with arthritis, his hands kept steady as he expertly plied his trade. His eyes and body were failing him, but his mind was as sharp as it had always been, and his heart was ever kind. Julie had more confidence in Arturo than in anyone else in St. Louis. She thought if anyone looked unwell, it was him.

The shop was dirty, as she expected, the stale air smelling of musty wood and old sawdust, but she had never known it to be any other way. She suspected that if anyone ever gave the place a thorough cleaning, it would probably collapse without all the dirt to hold it up. He still had several racks of music books and sheet music, and even sold a few of them occasionally, when some brave soul wandered in looking for a hard to find piece. No instruments were for sale any longer. The only instruments in the shop were those few being worked on. Most of them belonged to musicians who lived out of state and had their heavily insured violins, violas, cellos and bows shipped to Arturo, probably never realizing their precious cargo was going to such a deteriorated hell hole.

"Arturo, it is good to see you!" Julie walked up to the counter. "I can't wait to show you my new bow! What do you think?"

The old man took the bow from her, holding it expertly in his hands, turning it over, lightly bouncing it. He whistled softly. "Julie, this is exquisite workmanship. What a bow! But my eyes are so bad now. Help me here. Tell me the name on the bow. Who has made this? I'm afraid I can't see a name."

"I was hoping you could tell me," Julie replied, hiding her disappointment. "I couldn't find any identifying marks on it either. I was hoping to find out if I had a Peccatee or a Tourte. Oh, well," she sighed, "Whatever it is, it needs new hair."

"Julie, I believe this bow may be hand-made," Arturo said, his voice full of awe as he turned it over and ran his fingers along the wood. "Where did you say you got it?"

"Jack gave it to me after we had a really big fight. I was furious with him. It was his way of making things up to me."

A man with a mustache entered the shop and began to browse through the music books. Arturo and Julie continued their conversation.

"And then there was the plane crash," Arturo offered sympathetically. "I was sorry to hear about it. You poor child. But this bow he gave you is beautiful! What a precious memory for your husband to have left for you."

Yeah. That and the fact he was screwing my fake best friend and running an illegal arms business. With memories like that, I could use amnesia. Julie smiled at her elderly friend. Some things were better left unsaid.

"Well, then. Let's look and see, eh?" Arturo began unscrewing the nut to loosen the hair. As he twisted, the frog separated and a tiny round metal piece fell out of the nut, clinking softly on the counter top. "What do we have here?" he asked, puzzled, picking up the small disc.

Suddenly, there was a slight popping noise, and a blood spot appeared between Arturo's bewildered eyes. As Julie screamed, he fell backward to the floor. She whirled around to face the captain, whose gun was now aimed at her. Terror gripped her, holding her frozen. Before she could react, she was immediately amid a flurry of maelstrom. Thunderous noise echoed around her, seeming to come from everywhere, a rush of footsteps, the spray of gunfire, voices shouting. Julie felt as though she had been cut in two as searing pain ripped through her side. She fell to the floor, doubled over and lay in her own blood. *I'm going to die. Who are all these people? I'm dying. They killed Arturo. Help me, God. I'm going to die.*

"Julie! Julie! Stay with me. Hold on, honey, help is coming! Keisha!"

"The ambulance will be here shortly, Sam." Julie turned her head to see who had spoken. *That must be the woman who was at The Hall asking about me. Who is she?*

"Keisha called for back-up and medical help as soon as we saw the suspect entering the music shop," another man said. But they hadn't moved quickly enough, and now, Julie had been shot. It was too late for Arturo.

Julie felt herself drifting away. The pain was unbearable. *What is Sam doing here?* "Go away," she told him. "You betrayed me, too. You lied to me. Go away and leave me alone." *Can't you see I'm dying?* "Who are you, anyway? What's happening?" Her voice was weak and she struggled to stay conscious.

Sam held her head in his lap, ignoring her questions, begging her to hang on.

"The list…" Julie whispered. Her voice continued to weaken.

"Don't try to talk, Julie. Baby, just be still. You're gonna be okay. Stay with me now."

"The list...on the counter..." Julie blacked out.

Keisha Livingston hurried into Joe's office carrying a fresh stack of computer printouts. She could tell by the grim set of Joe's jaw that he was angry. This operation was not supposed to go down the way it did.

"Talk to me, Keisha. Our timing and that of the backup has already cost one innocent life, and another is hanging on slim hope. The suspect is dead, and my questions for him are now moot."

Keisha was keenly aware of how sobering the situation was. "I know you're upset, Joe. We all are and we're all pulling for Julie to make it through. But wait 'til you hear this!" She was excited to share the latest with her boss. "Joe, we got the head honcho. Bruno Meistermann in the flesh! He's also sometimes referred to as the captain. He was trained as a sharpshooter while serving in Germany's version of Black Ops forces and was unmatched for deadly accuracy. But, he received their equivalent of a dishonorable discharge when his psych eval indicated he was a psychopath. Interpol has a sheet a mile long on him. Cunning and cold-blooded, but never got his own hands dirty. He ran the entire organization and we got him! Why do you think he showed up himself, rather than sending in one of his henchmen?"

"Bruno Meistermann? No kidding! Everyone's after that guy. Feather in our cap. At this point, however, we can only surmise why he gave himself the assignment. We know that both Meistermann and the clients that Davenport ripped off were looking for that list, as were we. I guess after Jack took off and Meg failed him, he probably felt he was the most qualified if he wanted it done right. Arrogance rarely pays off. He took a big chance, and he lost. But I guess he was desperate to get his hands on that list and to try to track down the money before he ended up with a target on his head, so I guess he figured he was the only one he could trust. One less scumbag for us to worry about, but his clients may still be looking for Julie. Once we get everything off that disc, we should be able to make enough arrests to ensure her safety."

"Yeah, if she pulls through. Funny thing. Everybody thought Julie had the list, and while it turns out she did, she was the last one to know it. At least now we have it and *nobody knows we have it*, so we can start shutting this operation down."

"Right. You did a good job, Keisha. You were an important member of this team. Your significant contribution to this mission will be noted in your file. Next up, get that list distributed to Interpol, the FBI, the ATF home office, you know the drill. Let's see if everyone can do their job as quickly and quietly as possible. We still need to find Jack Davenport. He could be absolutely anywhere. If I were him, I would be far away on a very remote island, laying low. Wow! I can't believe we got Bruno Meistermann. One of the biggest arms dealers on the planet and he was hiding out in Pineview, Missouri, of all places. He tempered his excitement and sobered. "How's Ms. Davenport, have you heard?"

"Still in surgery," Keisha answered. "She's lost a lot of blood. Sam's at the hospital. He wants to be with her when she wakes up. If she wakes up. All I could find out was that she's not out of the woods yet."

16

Beeping sounds. What's beeping? Funny beat for a metronome. Hushed voices. Why are they whispering? Julie opened her eyes slightly. Everything was blurry. She closed her eyes and tried to think, but her thoughts were incoherent. *Why are there nurses? Are they angels? Is this real? Is this Heaven? Lots of people in white. Comfort? Somebody holding my hand? Where am I? OH! PAIN!*

Julie opened her eyes fully and looked around. The fog slowly began to lift. Still groggy, she began to remember fragments of the shooting. The pain brought her more fully awake. Sam was seated beside her bed, holding her hand, worry lines deeply etched into his face. *What is he doing here? Why was I afraid of him? Who is Sam Hernandez?* Julie winced. Instantly, Sam called to the nurse.

"She's in pain. Please give her something."

The nurse checked Julie's chart and nodded. She injected the much needed pain medication into Julie's IV, informed Sam that she would notify the doctor that Julie was conscious, and left.

Julie felt weak and woozy in spite of the pain ripping through her, but the medication soon began to take the edge off the pain.

"How do you feel, Julie?"

"What are you doing here?"

"Do you always answer a question with a question? Why did you run from me?"

"You lied to me. You are not a cop. The Pineview police have never heard of you. Who are you anyway? Why are you here?"

Sam took a deep breath. "My name is Sam Hernandez and I am here because I broke Rule Number Two."

"What?"

"Rule Number Two. I broke it."

"What are you talking about, Sam? What's Rule Number Two?"

"Rule Number Two is, never break Rule Number One."

She shot him an exasperated look. "I'm really tired, Sam. Arturo is dead. I'm tired. I hurt. I'm miserable. What's Rule Number One?"

"Rule Number One is never fall in love with a suspect."

"Go away. I didn't murder my husband. I didn't know he was selling arms. You're not a cop and you lied to me. Who *are* you? You at least owe me that much."

"Julie, I am Special Agent Samuel Hernandez with the ATF. Alcohol, Tobacco and Firearms. I'm sorry I kept that from you, but when you're better, I promise I'll tell you everything. We were investigating your husband and the organization he was involved with. They were dangerous arms dealers. Can I get you something? I never wanted you to get hurt. I was afraid you were going to die. The doctors worked a long time on you. We're the same blood type. I gave you your first and last pint of blood. I would have given you my last drop if they would have taken it.

"I'm sorry I couldn't tell you anything. I knew all along you were a victim, but officially, you were still a suspect. We'll talk about this later, when you're stronger. In the meantime, can I bring you anything? Anything at all?"

"My pets. And my chocolate."

"Honey, this is a hospital. No animals allowed. I'll take you home to see your pets as soon as possible. I don't even know where they are right now."

"They're in U. City at the Goldman's house." Julie's voice was growing weaker. "Stanley and Sheila don't know about any of this." She gave him the address and after he promised to take care of everything, Julie, surrendering to the pain medication, fell back asleep.

Sam, Joe and Keisha combed over autopsy reports and agent reports, discussing every detail of the incident at Arturo's shop.

"Not that this is exactly shocking, but the bullet that killed Arturo and the bullet that injured Julie were from the same gun used in the killings of Manny Tupelo and Meg Curtis. We don't have any evidence connecting that gun to any other crimes here in the States, so Bruno Meistermann did not kill indiscriminately. But Interpol may be interested in our findings," Joe offered.

"When will we get the results of Meistermann's autopsy?" Keisha asked.

Joe stifled a chuckle and answered, "Bruno Meistermann was shot full of bullets from several different weapons. It's going to take the coroner a while to determine exactly which bullet or bullets were responsible for actually causing his death. I'm just glad that an international criminal of his caliber has been removed. The world's a safer place for it, and we are much closer to closing this case."

"Agreed," Sam said firmly. "We have to be certain the bureau's files on this case are absolutely accurate and sealed. If the truth about what happened at Arturo's becomes public knowledge, our entire operation will be in jeopardy."

"How can we keep that quiet when a highly respected symphony cellist was taken by ambulance and hospitalized for a gunshot wound? How does that not reach the newspaper?"

"Fortunately, at least for us, that area is so crime ridden, we can hide it on a back page where it will just be another of several incidents that most folks won't even bother reading about. We will write the police report, so we control what is reported. It will be riddled with heavily edited information. It will just look like Julie was having her bow serviced when an armed robber interrupted. Robbery gone bad, nothing more. It'll be a one paragraph mention in the crime section of *The Post*, nothing more."

Sam thought Sheila was going to have a heart attack in front of him. He assured her Julie was out of danger, but needed rest and quiet while she recovered. For her safety, the hospital at which Julie was being treated was kept a secret. The Goldmans made him promise they would be the first to know where she was when she was able to have visitors. It was an easy promise for him to make because he knew he wouldn't have to keep it. He would not allow such a risk to be taken. He was aggravated at them for not coming forth with Julie's whereabouts when Keisha was questioning the symphony members, but he also understood their desire to protect Julie from certain danger. He took a photo of the pets to show Julie. That would have to placate her for a while. He decided the animals would be best cared for at the Medcalf's veterinary hospital, so he gathered the menagerie and dropped them off. Fred's stitches would come out before Julie's. He felt certain that she would prefer the Medcalfs board her crew, rather than the Goldmans.

He drove back to the hospital and found Julie sitting up in bed sipping broth. Her face was tear-streaked and her eyes were swollen from crying. Sam's heart broke for her. She didn't deserve any of this. He showed her the photo of her pets, and she seemed grateful he had taken the initiative to leave them in Pam and Mark's care. He held her hand. She began to cry fresh tears.

"He killed Arturo. My wonderful friend Arturo is dead because of me."

Sam stroked her arm, carefully avoiding the tubes. "Julie, I read the coroner's autopsy report on Arturo. Your bow was the last job Arturo would have performed, I'm afraid. I know this doesn't lessen the trauma you have just suffered, but Arturo was dying. He had at best only a few weeks to live. He was a very sick man and suffering."

Julie looked at Sam and cried silently, her tears running down her face and dampening the bed sheets. Would this nightmare ever end?

"You're alive, Julie. You survived an attempt on your life by a cold-blooded killer. I am sorry about Arturo. Our team was outside in the utility van and we started to move in as soon as that man entered the shop, but we were not fast enough. You need to concentrate on getting well."

"I lost an ovary. That will drastically reduce my chances of having children."

"You nearly lost your life. That reduces your chances even more."

"I always wanted children. It is very unlikely I can ever have any now."

"Julie, you need to focus on other things now. Like getting well and seeing your pets again."

"Did you get my chocolates?"

"You can't have solids yet. The chocolates will keep."

"What happens now?"

"First, you get better and get out of here. You have had a lot to deal with. You are safe for now, at any rate. There is an armed guard outside your door round the clock."

"I thought the gunman was shot when everyone stormed in. Meg is dead, that Tupelo guy is dead. I'm not understanding much, I guess."

"Julie, I will explain everything to you when you're stronger. For now, can we just try to get better and let everything else go?"

"I suppose you haven't told me everything, huh?"

You don't know the half of it. You're not even the widow you think you are, but if I find him first, you will be. He gently squeezed her hand. "When you are strong and healthy, I will tell you everything, okay?"

"Right."

"Don't worry about anything. Don't worry about having children. Don't worry about your pets, your house, or your safety."

"Su Li will call me. I had a dream about Miyso. She was happy and healthy. It was such a good dream. She was fine and we were all laughing and talking together."

Sam sighed. He had hoped to postpone this conversation. Julie looked so fragile, he wondered if she could take any more. He spoke softly to her, still holding her hand.

"Don't worry about Su Li. I tracked her down in California and told her you had been in a little accident, but you were being cared for. It's an understatement, admittedly, but her mother passed away last night while you were in surgery, so Su Li will be coming home in a few more days. I will meet her at the airport and fill her in, but there's no point in causing her more grief and angst at this time. I know that Miyso's passing is one more tragedy for you to deal with, and I am sorry for yet another loss. Please, get some sleep. I will take care of everything. I promise. I am so sorry this has happened to you."

"Thank you, Sam. I'm sorry I was mad at you. Thank you for taking care of Johann, Sebastienne, and Fred."

He brushed her hair back with his hand and kissed her lightly on top of her head. "Get some rest. I will get you out of here as soon as you are well enough."

She pumped the pain killer to the maximum dosage, closed her eyes and drifted to sleep.

17

Kendra Grady sat on the deck of the modest home she shared with her husband of nearly thirty years. She remained motionless, a statue, deep in thought. Judson watched her from the kitchen. She did not appear to be praying or reading her Bible, which sat unopened on the table in front of her next to the morning paper. Eventually, curiosity prevailed and he quietly approached her. "I'd offer you a penny for your thoughts, but I have a feeling they might be worth much more. What are you so concerned about?"

She looked up at her husband and smiled slightly. He was a wise and perceptive man, well suited to shepherd a church. Their marriage had been mostly happy, sometimes filled with trials and disappointment, yet each difficulty they weathered brought them closer to each other, and closer to the God they served. She loved and admired Judson Grady more than any man she knew, and was relieved to share her thoughts with him now.

"Did you see the paper?"

"Not yet. Why?"

"There was a shooting. Julie Davenport, that troubled lady who donated all those beautiful clothes to the church was a victim."

"No! Oh, no! God has put that woman on my mind for a while. I have been burdened to keep her in prayer. Did she survive? Does it say what hospital she is in?"

"No," she replied, puzzled. "The entire article is vague and sketchy. You would think that a woman of her stature would have garnered a little more press. I was wondering if we might be able to find out."

"I'll check the service list to see which of our deacons will be doing hospital visitation today. Maybe we can learn where she is." Pastor Grady picked up the phone and began to dial.

Pineview Community Church had a congregation whose ages ranged from birth to 98 years. Generally, several members of his congregation would be in the various area hospitals at any given time, for a myriad of reasons; giving birth, accidents, heart attacks, you name it. Hospital visitation was a busy ministry, involving a rotating schedule of deacons, pastoral staff, and their wives.

"I have wondered if she wasn't involved in something dangerous or even illegal. The same week she brought in her late husband's clothes, the church had a break-in, remember? Only nothing was taken. It was so odd, because only those boxes which she had donated had been searched, as if the person was looking for something. And now, she is a shooting victim in a rough neighborhood."

He nodded, agreeing that the circumstances of the break-in were unusual, but as nothing they could ascertain had been stolen, they did not bother to call the police. He retreated to the kitchen to finish his calls, and told Kendra to keep praying for Julie, and they would wait to see if they could learn more. Before he left her, he rubbed her neck and kissed the top of her head. "I'll be in my study preparing Sunday's sermon. I'll let you know if I hear anything. We mustn't worry. Only trust. God always knows what He is doing. On rare occasions, He clues us in." She smiled broadly, and he winked at her with a twinkle in his eye. That was one of her husband's favorite sayings.

Within the hour, Judson Grady's phone rang. He found Kendra in the kitchen. "Danny just called. He's visiting at St. Luke's. He said the information desk did not have Julie Davenport registered, but he also said that one of the rooms in the private

wing had an armed guard sitting outside the door. Now, while
I'm not a betting man—"

"Judson, that's got to be her. Do you think you can go see
her?"

He was already picking up his car keys.

The guard on duty outside Julie's hospital room called a nurse
and asked her to find out if Julie wanted to see Pastor Grady.
The guard would not leave his post. Julie had had no visitors
other than Sam, and none were expected. Any visitors had to be
cleared before being allowed in. In the meantime, he examined
Judson Grady's identification and called Joe for a background
check and approval before allowing the pastor entrance to Julie's
room. Eventually, Judson Grady was allowed to see her, but the
door would remain open.

Julie looked up at Pastor Grady with eyes that reminded him
of an abandoned puppy.

"Hi." Her soft voice resounded with defeat and grief. She had
been crying and was in pain, so he would keep the visit short.

"Julie, we were sorry to hear about what happened. I came to
see how you were doing and to ask if we might pray together."

"I don't think God is all that concerned about me." She waited
for him to object, but he stayed quiet, so she continued. "I don't
understand why all of this is happening. Do you know I will
probably never even be able to have children? Why would God
allow this if He loves me so much?"

"Julie, nobody knows the future. Nobody can say what will
or will not happen. It is in God's hands. And those are the most
capable hands I know. You ask why there is evil in the world,
if God is a God of love. I cannot tell you why anything at all
happens. Why is there good in the world? Why do people reach
out to total strangers to help them in their time of need? Why do

flowers bring us joy? You can't question why there is evil in the world, and not at the same time, question why there is good, or why miracles happen. These are questions that I think are best discussed when you are stronger, so maybe we can revisit those concerns once you are well. I do know that the greater the evil that happens, the greater the good that God can bring out of it. I do know that in our hour of darkest need, God is there to comfort us, to be present, and to show His love to us. I do know that you can trust Him with your whole life. Once you do, you can know that He will always be there with you, not to keep anything bad from happening to you, but to carry you through the bad times when they come.

"He allowed His only Son to suffer and die at the hands of evil men. God's heart is grieved when people choose evil. But He gave us a free will to make choices. Every choice has a consequence, and many times, it is the innocent who suffer. It certainly looks that way in your case. But He will always be there for you, if you only ask Him. You have to make the choice to trust Him. Let God be God, Julie. One of my favorite verses in the Bible says, 'Be still and know that I am God.' Sometimes, that is the only thing I can repeat to myself. When things seem so out of control, I meditate on that verse. And it brings me peace."

Julie remained silent, but nodded her head.

"Julie, we will be praying for you. Is there anything our church can do for you?"

"No. I guess I'll take the prayers. Thank you for coming to see me. And for caring. I appreciate it."

Pastor Grady prayed with Julie briefly and took his leave.

18

"Su Li Tuan? I'm Special Agent Sam Hernandez with the ATF. I spoke with you on the phone a few days ago about Julie." Sam recognized Su Li as soon as she deplaned. He had seen dozens of photographs of her and Julie together from their childhood to the present. She looked tired and sad and he was not about to make her day any brighter.

"What has happened, Agent Hernandez? How is Julie? What's going on?"

"Please, call me Sam. May I drive you home? I just got Julie settled in at the house. She didn't want to burden you any more than you already were. Why don't we talk on the way home? Let's get your baggage."

Su Li was too tired to raise any protest. She was uneasy and puzzled that a federal agent had met her at the airport, and was wondering what in the world had happened since she left for California.

Sam filled Su Li in on all that had transpired in her absence. She listened quietly, trying to fathom all he was saying. It sounded too fantastic to believe. How could Julie not have told her any of this? She had known all along that Meg was not to be trusted, but was shocked to hear that Meg and Jack were involved in arms dealing, and with each other. How could Julie survive such an ordeal alone?

"So she's going to be okay? She's home alone now?"

"She will be fine, but she is still pretty weak. It is not safe for her to be alone until we have apprehended all the suspects who remain a threat to her. We also need to find Jack Davenport and bring him to justice."

"Wow. Frosting on the cake. This is all pretty hard to believe. Is she able to care for the animals?"

"They are still at the vet's. I was hoping we could pick them up on the way back, if you can handle it. I know you've just suffered your own loss, and I don't want to burden you further."

Su Li managed a laugh. "No problem. I pretty much do everything around there anyway. I love those fur balls as much as she does. Julie and I have been together since we were children. I have always watched out for her. Jack had me fooled as well, I guess. How did she take the news that he was still alive?"

It was Sam's turn to chuckle. "How do you think?" They both laughed together and the mood lightened.

"How'd she do with the redecorating? That's not really her thing. She really loved that place when Jack built it for her, but now, I guess all that's tainted, huh?"

"Actually, she stayed with the same color scheme. It doesn't look all that different, but you will notice some changes. She's gonna be very happy to see you. She has missed you a lot."

They arrived at Medcalf Animal Hospital. Fred was overjoyed to see Su Li, who instructed Pam Medcalf to send Julie the bill. They piled the furry crew into the car and headed home.

Julie and Su Li hugged tightly and cried. Miyso's suffering had ended, but her loss was deeply felt. Julie was weak, as Sam indicated, but happy to have her friend and her pets home.

Sam explained to the women that until he and Joe determined they were safe, there would be a 24 hour guard on them. Holding up his hand as they began to object, he firmly said, "Julie, this is not up for discussion. I nearly lost you once. Your safety is my number one priority."

Su Li shot a questioning glance at her friend. Apparently a few details of recent events had been left out. Julie blushed and mouthed "later" to Su Li, who stood and started for the kitchen.

"Well, I am certain you haven't cooked anything more difficult than a bowl of Cocoa Puffs. I will make you bone marrow soup which will aid the healing process, so you can get back on your feet and back on your cello. The world at large is missing out on beautiful music. At some point, you're going to run out of leave time at the symphony, and you'll be job hunting once more, something I never intend to go through again, so I will take extra good care of you so you can get back to work. I've become accustomed to living here in grand style, and I'm not moving. Bone marrow soup coming up!" Su Li was once again in charge of the kitchen and was wasting no time taking charge of Julie's care.

"I hate that stuff, Su Li. Pizza sounds much better. Let's order."

"Bone marrow soup. For healing. No arguing." She marched into the kitchen calling out that she would bring tea once the soup was on the stove.

"So what's in it?" Sam asked Julie.

"Don't ask. Ancient Vietnamese recipe for healing everything, if the taste doesn't kill you first. Anyway, it takes a long time to make, so we might as well order pizza while we wait."

Sam laughed and put up his hands defensively. "Oh, no! I am not getting into the middle of this."

Julie changed the subject. "Sam, I feel really safe when you're here, so please don't take this wrong, but how long do you think this is going to go on? Su Li is right. I will have to return to work soon if I want to keep my position. The symphony has been more than generous with me."

"It's an international case, Julie, and we are making excellent progress. Finding that list the way we did, with no witnesses to leak information, means that nobody on the list knows they've been identified. Arrests are being made almost daily on four continents, and with each arrest, the suspects have been caught by surprise. It shouldn't be too much longer before we've got them all rounded up. When the bureau believes you are safe, the guard will be removed, and our case file on this matter will be closed."

He paused and studied his hands before continuing. "Which brings me to another subject."

"You'll be leaving Pineview."

"I'll be leaving Pineview, but I still live and work in St. Louis. I will be happy to close this case, but…I would be even happier if you would agree to continue seeing me." Sam seemed to struggle for the first time, to express his thoughts. He hesitated, and began, "I realize you may have some trust issues after all that's happened—"

"I'll still see you," she interrupted.

Sam squeezed her hand and pressed it to his lips. "Good."

19

Back at the St. Louis office, Keisha Livingston placed a stack of paperwork in front of Sam. "I wrote your reports for you. I know you have been busy watching your charge, along with bringing in groceries and all. Going just a tad over and above the call of duty I'd say." Keisha was obvious about letting Sam know she didn't approve of his breaking Rule Number Two, but she was still willing to pull his load for him. She was not about to stand in the way of love, regardless of the circumstances that sparked it. "If you'll just review these reports and sign off on them, then the bureau won't be waiting to finalize the closing of the case."

"Thanks, Keisha. You've been a huge help. I see a promotion in your very near future."

She flashed Sam a big, toothy smile. Working this case was her dream. It had been challenging and there were times she was not certain she was the best fit, so she considered the kudos from Sam and Joe to be high praise indeed. "It's been a pleasure working with you and Joe. I hope we can be a team again in the future."

"Count on it."

"Hi, Terry, it's Julie Davenport. So do I still have a job? And thanks for the flowers. They are gorgeous."

"Hey, Jules. Good to hear your voice. You're sounding much stronger. When will you be back?"

"I have my final follow-up with the doc on Thursday, and if it's all good, I should be back at The Hall on Monday. I have been able to practice for the past three weeks, and I feel ready to come back. I'm not all that certain as to where I stand with my leave, and I just wanted to be sure there was a job to come back to."

"Julie, up until Jack died, you had never taken any vacation, sick leave, nothing, other than when your parents died. Funeral leave doesn't count if you miss a week or less. You're good, but I hope you stay healthy for a year, so you can build time back up again. Not to mention, you can always claim extenuating circumstances. No one could argue with that."

"Su Li is back, so I've been relegated to a healthy diet once more. It'll be great to get back to work."

"You bet. I will put you back on starting Monday, unless you tell me differently. Thanks for calling. Oh, and please give Stanley and Sheila a call."

"Will do. Driving you nuts?"

"Yep."

Julie hung up. She was looking forward to returning to work. As much as she enjoyed Sam's company when he was on duty, she and Su Li were feeling like prisoners in their home. She was feeling strong and had worked hard at overcoming the victim mentality that set in after recent events. She was a victor, not a victim. She had survived and those who wished her harm had not.

She looked around her spacious living room, bright and fragrant after word got out that she had been shot in an armed robbery at Arturo's. ATF spin control was convincing, if not entirely accurate. There were flowers from the symphony organization as well as some of its individual members, flowers from some of the symphony's corporate sponsors, flowers from the Medcalfs, flowers from Sam, even flowers from Keisha and Joe. Wanh sent a lovely floral arrangement, and Pineview Community Church delivered flowers and a week's worth of delicious casseroles. The Goldmans sent numerous teddy bears with flowers and balloons with flowers. Julie felt loved and deeply grateful for the support and kindness shown by so many. She was also grateful that neither she nor Su Li suffered from flower allergies.

She called the Goldmans to let them know she intended to return to work on Monday, news they were delighted to hear.

20

"What are you thinking? You can't be serious! We don't know she is out of danger. How can you do this?" Sam was angry and not afraid to show it. He was in the St. Louis office turning in the last of the paperwork Keisha had been kind enough to prepare.

Captain Carlton Drake was unmoved. There were other cases to work and he had neither the time, nor the inclination to argue with Sam Hernandez. "Sam, the bureau cannot keep guarding that place forever. The names on the list have been arrested. Bruno Meistermann is dead, and what's left of his organization is scattered without their leader. There is no longer any apparent threat to Ms. Davenport. It is neither financially, nor practically feasible to continue protection."

"Jack Davenport is still out there," Sam countered.

"The chances of Jack Davenport being anywhere near Pineview are slim to none. Besides that, as far as he knows, Julie thinks he's dead. He has no motive to harm her, but every motive under the sun to get as far away from Pineview as possible. Now, you and your team have worked continuously 'round the clock and you have all done an outstanding job. This was a big win and I know you're tired. I am giving all three of you two weeks off for R and R, but after that, you'll have a new assignment. Our part of this case is closed with the notation that Jack Davenport is still at large somewhere on the planet. If we ever get a lead on

Davenport, we'll follow it up at that time, but there is no reason to continue our work in Pineview. Joe was on duty out there now, and I have just called him in. Keisha has already booked a flight to Baltimore to visit her family. Sam, you've gotten too close to this case, something you've never done before, and it has clouded your judgment. Take your two weeks. Take more if you want to use your earned vacation time, but come back refreshed and ready to work. We have no shortage of other cases piling up." Captain Drake did not wait for a reply. His orders having been issued, he turned and retreated to his office.

Sam sped out to Julie's home, Captain Drake's words playing over in his mind. He tried to be objective. The captain's reasoning sounded sane enough, but Sam's gut was churning with uncertainty. Maybe his feelings for Julie were clouding his judgment after all. He had never allowed the lines to blur between personal and professional in his career, but he had also never been so crazy about one woman before either. *She's quirky and different, that's for sure.* He considered what a future might be like with someone who was used to the finer things in life. He knew he could not provide for her the way the great Jack Davenport had. How important would that be to her? On the flip side, he also knew that Jack Davenport could not love her as he did. Money didn't seem all that important to her, but then, she had never been without enough. He had sworn off relationships after the divorce. They were messy and never worth the trouble. But knowing Julie was making him rethink the wisdom in that decision. Still, he was afraid for her safety. *Am I overreacting?*

He picked up his cell phone and called her. Joe was gone, never questioning the wisdom of Captain Drake's order, and Julie and Su Li were home alone with the animals.

"We're fine, Sam. You worry too much. Su Li is cooking up a storm in the kitchen. It's great to have her back, and now, life can at least get back to some semblance of normal. I'm glad you're coming over. You can join us for a scrumptious dinner. Now I can stop being your case and start seeing where we end up. Doesn't that sound lovely?"

Sam relaxed and smiled. It did sound lovely. And Julie sounded good—cheerful, upbeat, strong. He slowed his pace and told her he would be there in a few more minutes. He turned off the highway and continued traveling the now familiar winding roads toward Julie's home. For the first time since coming to Pineview, Sam allowed himself to admire the beauty of the intricate creation that was abundant in this area. The flowers, the tree covered hills, the foliage that graced every inch of ground, beckoned with the promise of a serene existence. He could see the draw in living out here, far removed from the city, pollution, smog, and people. It was a peaceful drive surrounded by lush greenery and delicate wildflowers. Pineview meant a long commute for Julie, but she seemed willing enough to make it. It was worth the drive, he supposed, if you came home to a setting such as this.

Rounding the last curve, he turned up the road leading to her driveway. A white delivery van was pulling in under the canopy, just ahead of him, piquing his curiosity. He watched as the driver, clad in a navy blue jump suit and matching cap, retrieved a large arrangement of flowers and headed for the front door. Sam silently pulled into the driveway and quietly followed directly behind the deliveryman as Su Li opened the door and ushered him in. More flowers. Just what Julie needed. Fred, ever at attention, growled, then wagged his tail as Julie called to him and rose to accept yet another arrangement of flowers.

A loud shot suddenly echoed through the house and the deliveryman crumpled to the floor, dropping the vase, shattering it. Blood and water mingled over the recently replaced carpet. Julie screamed and recoiled and looked up terrified at Sam, who stood holding his revolver.

"What the—! Sam! What are you doing! You killed this man! You shot him in the back! What are you thinking! What's *wrong* with you!" She was near hysteria. Su Li looked on in horrified shock, her eyes wide, both hands covering her mouth.

Sam coolly walked over to the body, rolled it over with his foot and kicked off the man's cap. "You are now officially a widow,

Julie," he said calmly, as Jack Davenport's unseeing eyes gazed into nothing. Underneath the flowers haphazardly strewn all over the floor, Sam kicked out a knife that Jack had carefully concealed. "*Now* the case is closed."

For nearly a full minute, there was complete silence as the women stared at Jack and his weapon, taking everything in. Then, in a unified chorus, Julie and Su Li both asked in amazement, "How did you know?"

Julie continued, "His back was to you the entire time, and his cap was pulled down. You had no way of knowing it was Jack."

Sam was as matter-of-fact as she had ever seen him. "Julie, you're going back to work Monday. Why would anyone besides me, of course, send you flowers for no reason, and especially when you're well enough to return to work? And who was even left to send you flowers? Your social circle is pretty small and as it is, your house is starting to look and smell like a funeral parlor. The very idea that you would at this time get flowers is suspicious, don't you think?"

It was obvious that Julie was not buying Sam's explanation. "That's pretty sketchy. I know you're good, Sam, or you wouldn't be doing what you do. You had to be certain or you would never have shot him. So how did you know this guy was Jack?"

Sam looked around, as though the walls or furniture might provide an answer, but they weren't talking. He hated to give credit to someone else, but the truth would have to come out. "While I would like to tell you that it's because of my superior detecting skills, I'm afraid that would be untrue." He paused and then confessed, "Somebody told me."

"Somebody told you that Jack would be delivering flowers, and you didn't tell your captain to keep the protection detail on us? Why would you do that, Sam?"

"No. That's not what they told me. I didn't know before I got here. They told me the deliveryman was Jack right before I shot him." He was starting to fidget.

Julie remained skeptical, crossing her arms in front of her chest, her eyebrows raised. "Oh that makes perfect sense," she said sarcastically. "Su Li and I were the only ones here. Did you know, Su Li? You let him in."

Su Li's eyes widened. "No, no! Of course not!" she exclaimed. "I did not get a good look at him behind the flowers. I had no idea. Sam, how could you accuse me of such a thing!"

Women. Sam rolled his eyes. "No, Su Li did not know either."

"Kind of running out of possibilities here, Sam. How were you so entirely positive this guy was Jack, that you risked shooting him in the back right in front of both of us?"

Sam sighed in resignation. "Fred told me, okay?"

Su Li looked suspiciously at Sam, but Julie threw her arms around Fred, then Sam.

"Of course! How could I be so dense? I should have known the second he wagged his tail. He recognized Jack, before I called him over to me. Fred is never welcoming to strangers."

"I well remember," Sam offered. "If he doesn't know you, he isn't happy to see you."

"Steak dinner for Fred tonight."

"Hey, what about me?" Sam asked, feigning dramatic hurt.

"Well, I guess you were the ultimate hero since you picked up on it so quickly. Steak dinner for you, too." Julie became instantly calm, as if they were discussing the benefits of solar energy. Sam thought she seemed too quickly recovered and back to business as usual, while Jack's lifeless body lay between them.

"Julie, honey, are you okay? I mean, you know, just when you thought it was safe to go back in the water and all that?" He was concerned that she seemed entirely unaffected by the fact that Jack had returned to kill her, and was instead, lying dead on her floor.

"Never better." Julie sounded strong, cool, and confident.

He threw her a questioning look.

"Sam, Jack was dead to me once, and I mourned and grieved until I was reduced to a mere shadow of myself. Then, I learned of his betrayal, not only with a person I thought was a friend, but also in the ways he was using me. He died to me again, only that time, I didn't grieve anything besides my own gullibility. Now, he's dead for real. I guess the third time's a charm."

"Su Li? How are you?" Sam asked, still not comprehending Julie's matter-of-fact demeanor.

"I'm with Julie," she replied in casual agreement, dismissing his concern. "I've seen worse."

Sam shook his head. He supposed he would have to get used to this.

"Well, I need to secure the scene and call this in. Why don't you ladies retreat to the hearth room and I will join you soon. Su Li, a nice pot of tea would be most appreciated, if you feel up to it. Thanks." He would have preferred something much stronger, but it was bad form to have alcohol on your breath when the crime scene investigators showed up. "Julie, you will need to secure the animals away from the living room. Better put Fred someplace where he can't intimidate the investigators."

Sam taped off the living room so as not to disturb the evidence and joined the women in the hearth room to wait for the crime crew for what he hoped would be the final time at this address.

Su Li served tea and the three of them sat together talking, as though chatting and sipping tea in the hearth room with a dead body in the living room was a normal every day activity.

"Julie, the one thing I don't get, is why would he come here to kill you? You posed no threat to him, and as far as he knew, you thought he was dead. Captain Drake stressed that point when he cancelled the protection detail. I cannot figure out what Jack could possibly gain from your death."

Julie shrugged nonchalantly. "I guess the money. That's all I can think of."

"What money? Do you know what he did with the money he stole? *Do you know where it is?*"

"Good lord, no. No clue in the world. I mean *my* money."

"I thought Jack was the one who spent so lavishly on you and kept you in a lifestyle most women would love to become accustomed to?"

"I do work, you know. The symphony pay check is a cut or two above flipping burgers."

"Honey, I know what you make. Quite a bit more than I do, but not enough for this kind of lifestyle. I know you collected the life insurance, but when we checked into your finances, you hadn't even touched it. However, Jack had no access to your accounts."

"No, not that money. My trust fund."

"You have a trust fund? Why on earth are you even working?"

"Sam, I work because I reach people with my music. It is satisfying to practice and practice a challenging piece, to master it, to perform it, and to touch people's hearts with it. I was born to do this. It's not just a career, it's a calling. To do something less would be a failure to fulfill my purpose in life." She went on to explain, "I'm the sole beneficiary of my father's trust fund. He was a prominent and very wealthy surgeon. After my mother died, he wanted to be sure I was well provided for. You never know what might happen that could end your career. But I have never touched that money. At least, not so far. When Jack and I got married, I changed the ownership of the trust to benefit us jointly.

"Of course, there is a generous provision for Su Li, so Jack did not come here to kill only me. He would have had to get rid of her as well if he wanted it all."

"It would have taken him mere seconds to kill you both with that knife he brought. Julie, didn't you consult your attorney before you made such a drastic change to your trust?"

"Oh yeah. He was dead set against it. Tried every way possible to talk me out of it. He's been our trusted family attorney for years, but I told him if he wouldn't draw up the papers, I would find someone who would. He warned me, but I didn't listen to him."

"Yeah, I noticed that's a habit with you."

"Sam, I believe marriage is for a lifetime, and if you're in, you're in all the way. Jack was my husband and I thought it was wrong to keep anything from him. He had plenty of money of his own. At least it certainly appeared so. I never dreamed something like this could happen."

"Why didn't you tell me any of this?"

Julie smiled and raised her eyebrows. "You never asked."

Sam leaned back in his chair and sighed. "Does anybody else know about the trust fund?"

"Nope. People treat you differently if they know you have money. Besides, I don't think it's anybody's business. Su Li didn't even know until now."

"Okay. I think I hear the crime van. Why don't you both stay in here while I go outside?" Sam left the room resignedly, shaking his head, as if somehow, that would help him understand the unfathomable Julie Davenport.

"He's really cute when he's exasperated with you," Su Li whispered.

"I heard that," Sam called back over his shoulder. They collapsed into giggles.

Sam returned several minutes later, carrying a clipboard. "Julie, did you know whether there was a life insurance policy on you?"

"No. There really wasn't any need. The only people I had to leave money to were Jack and Su Li, and they had promised to take care of any animals I had, so the trust fund was available."

Sam removed papers from the clipboard. "Then you knew nothing about a policy insuring your life for five million dollars naming Jack the sole beneficiary?"

"Five million dollars! I only got two mil when he died. The first time, I mean. And no, I was not aware. I guess he was covering all his bases, huh? Jack had very expensive taste. It required a great deal of money to keep him happy."

"Yeah. Looks like he had several million motives for murder. It's gonna be a while before you can go back into your living room. They're still cleaning up in there. I gotta admit, it was kind of fun watching Captain Drake eat his words. I'm relieved this nightmare is finally over for you, babe."

"That makes two of us."

"Three of us," Su Li chimed in.

21

One year later

"Baby, I'm home. Dinner smells good! What did Su Li fix to-night?"

Julie glided deftly to Sam to greet him with a kiss. "A very special dinner, just for us. Su Li is out tonight, so I cooked dinner all by my lonesome. So how was your day? Did my big, strong husband catch any bad guys today?"

He pulled her to him and kissed her warmly, happy she hadn't burned the house down. "I missed you. And you look absolutely beautiful tonight. Awfully dressed up for dinner at home," he commented, admiring the effect of her long, flowing apricot colored evening gown. "How was your corporate concert this afternoon? Didn't you have a meet and greet? I thought you'd be home later."

"I bugged out as soon as the concert was over. I wanted to come home and be sure your special dinner was just perfect."

Sam laughed at the idea of his wife in the kitchen. He sat down. The table was set with candles, china, and the good silverware. Something was up.

"Okay, Julie. I'll bite. What's the deal here?"

She served him his dinner plate, arranged with shrimp, baby carrots, baby asparagus, and mini tacos and smiled.

"Uh. Pretty sure Su Li didn't think this dinner up."

"Nope. This was my idea."

"Okay," he answered, more confused than ever. "It's kind of an unusual meal, don't you think?"

She smiled sweetly. "No. It's not unusual. It's special."

"It's so special, you forgot the wine."

"No. I didn't forget the wine. You can have some wine if you like."

"Probably a good idea to wash this stuff down with. What kind do you want?"

"Oh, I won't be drinking any wine."

"Seriously? Why not?" The words were barely out of Sam's mouth, when he figured it all out. "Oh! Oh! Oh, Julie, honey! Really?" Sam jumped up and hugged her tightly, his eyes glistening.

"Yep."

"Do I at least know before Su Li?"

"Yep. But she's smart. She'll figure it out pretty soon."

"Have you already told Johann, Sebastienne, and Fred they're going to have a little brother or sister?"

"No, not yet. I thought we ought to do that together."

A Note from the Author

I originally began writing Unharmonious more than twenty years ago, but—life got in the way, and before I finished the book, it ended up on the back shelf, so to say, where it gathered dust, and became an increasingly fading dream. I have always loved writing and hoped that when that magical "someday" arrived, I would finish my book. In the meantime, I ghost wrote and edited for other writers, until finally, my husband cornered me and said, "You have helped other people with their books. When are you going to finish yours?" As is occasionally the case, he was right. So the laundry piled up, cooking was often sacrificed, the house got dusty and we lived to tell about it.

Unharmonious takes place in the early to mid 1990s. The world was simpler then. The digital invasion had not arrived. The terrorist attacks of September 11 were unimaginable. Cell phones and home computers, while not unheard of, were not common. People *talked* to each other without using their thumbs at breakneck speed. And while life was far from idyllic, it was not the frenetic race to nowhere that has overtaken much of our culture, risking our ability to experience the joy of deep friendship.

Unharmonious takes place in and around St. Louis. Why St. Louis? It's a great place to live and visit; rich in culture and history, great restaurants, interesting people, diverse yet friendly, and more things to do than one book could ever cover. Often described as a small town overgrown, it's a good place to raise a family. But one thing we all agree on—nobody moves here for the weather.

This book reflects a few of my great passions, special gifts I think God must have created, not only as one of many reflections of His glory, but also to enrich our lives and augment our joy. I have always loved music. My parents set me on their piano bench as soon as I was out of diapers. When I was four, they discovered I had perfect pitch and could name as many as eleven notes played simultaneously, so they further encouraged my interest in music. By the time I was ten, I played piano, cello, and guitar. As I got older, I sang in small and large groups, soloed, and spent twelve years singing with the St. Louis Metro Singers, who at that time, was the principal pops chorus for the St. Louis Symphony Orchestra. So it was easy for me to write about the beautiful Powell Hall and the thrill of performing there for many years.

I also have a deep love for animals. I cannot encourage people enough to adopt from shelters and bask in the grateful companionship of a loyal furry friend. I believe pets add much more to our lives than we can ever add to theirs. In this as well as my future books, they play an important role.

My love for good books goes without question. While I write both fiction and non-fiction, a page-turning mystery is just plain fun to read, and to write. I hope that you, dear reader, enjoy reading this book as much as I enjoyed writing it. If you have, please take a moment to leave a review. Reviews are the lifeblood of a book and your thoughts are warmly welcomed. Finally, if you would like to connect with me, you can find me at www.

laineboyd.com or on Facebook. I look forward to hearing from you.

~Laine

Dinner and a Murder

The original crime -- September 15, 1866

A silver crescent moon hung over St. Louis, its shimmery light largely obscured by gathering storm clouds, pregnant with the threat of rain. Captain Josiah Mansford quietly slipped off of his ship, the Mississippi Jewel, and into the shadows along the mighty river. Looking around to see if he had been observed, he was confident his movements had gone unnoticed by anyone on the docks. He stealthily crept into the forest, and hid among the trees, watching.

The pale moonlight provided sufficient illumination to check his pocket watch. The Jewel would not cast off until dawn, another two hours or so. Enough time, if he was careful. He had made certain that he was seen in several places on the ship before he left. If asked, a number of crewmen and staff could honestly swear they had seen him. But he also had a back-up plan. Good to have two explanations if one didn't work out. He hurried deeper into the woods to where he had left Sultana, his fastest Arabian mare, tied to a tree. He quickly mounted the jet black steed, and kicking her into a gallop, sped furiously toward home.

The rain began, first as a light drizzle, but steadily increasing, as thunder clapped and lightening sparked across the sky, frightening the horse. But Josiah, an expert rider, urged her on before stopping almost a quarter-mile from his home. He dismounted and tied her once again, firmly to an enormous tree where its abundant foliage and long, low branches would keep her dry from the coming storm. He moved furtively toward his home and silently entered through the kitchen door at the back of the house. He paused to steady his breathing. Josiah was a large man to begin with, but now forty-four years old, he was feeling his age, and the expanding girth that accompanied it hampered his efforts to move as quickly as he did when he was younger. He smoothed his gray beard. It was damp, as was his uniform. There would be no time to dry himself by the comfort of a warm fire. He would have to return to the Mississippi Jewel as soon as he was finished with the business at hand.

He crept up the servant's narrow staircase at the back of the house, avoiding the steps with the creaky boards, and listened intently. The servants' quarters were on the third floor of his home. The servants, at least those he had not fired recently, were sleeping. The house was quiet. He carefully entered the bedroom of Mrs. Anderson, the housekeeper. She lay on her back, snoring lightly, and did not stir as he walked noiselessly to her bed. Her gray curls fell haplessly from beneath her nightcap as she slept, unaware of Captain Mansford's presence. Taking a pillow, Josiah Mansford muffled his pistol and pressing it to her ample chest, shot her through her treacherous heart with barely more than a faint popping sound from his weapon. Her bright blue eyes opened widely as if in surprise and her head rose slightly from her pillow, then her eyes closed as her head fell back again, her tight gray curls bouncing one final time against her pillow.

It served her right, the lousy mick. She had known about the deception and had hidden it from him. That made her a most disloyal employee. He should have known better than to trust an

Irishwoman. He had taken pity on her with her sad tale of losing her husband and hired her to supervise the house staff. She was unworthy of the position, having chosen to keep his wife's dirty, little secret from him. Josiah narrowed his steel blue eyes and set his jaw in grim satisfaction that one traitor in his household had been easily eliminated. He would not tolerate disloyalty. They would pay. They would *all* pay.

"Dinner and a Murder" by Laine Boyd. Coming soon…

15151488R00132

Made in the USA
San Bernardino, CA
16 September 2014